THE FORGOTTEN KEYCHAINS

(THE FORGOTTEN SERIES)

Book 1

A novel by Julian Kennedy

This book is dedicated to my spouse that supports me through everything and the fierce, brave children we made together. You are my reason for healing and the driving force behind me finding myself again—and for the first time.

CONTENT WARNING

Again, this book contains references to rape, LGBTQ+ family issues, violence, and alcohol/narcotics misuse. Read with that in mind.

Table of Contents

Prologue

Several years earlier

I recognize the sound of his voice before I can even see him clearly. Obviously, I know he has issues but this is beyond the pale, and I can't stop shaking, especially the nearer he gets to me. "Holy shit. What's going on?" I ask.

"Hello," is all he says in return. Trembling, I lie on the old metal framed bed, and the posts creak every time I move. The sheets underneath me smell like they've spent years being unwashed. It's disgusting, like being trapped in my worst nightmare, like being trapped inside my own coffin. I don't know how I got here. Or when. It could have been hours ago. The memories feel dark and fuzzy. He must have dragged me here somehow. So why didn't I fight back?

A bead of sweat rolls down my forehead joining the collection of them forming on my upper lip. It's impossible to stop them from cascading down my chin and into the crevice of my collarbone. If the *surface of the sun* was a room temperature setting, that's what this asshole has it set on. Even if I could manage it I don't have the strength to wipe the sweat away. I feel dizzy, disoriented. Where the hell am I? The bed doesn't feel familiar, and the comforter is stiff, quilted, and itchy. I know I'm not at home.

The obvious answer is that he drugged me and brought me here, but I don't have any way of knowing unless I ask which I'm currently too scared to do. Or maybe if he brings it up, but he isn't saying much.

It takes a minute or two before I'm able to clearly see the person in front of me, and I'm still shocked even after hearing his voice. From what I can see, he's standing over me smiling and baring his teeth like a rabid dog. He bites his lip and greets me again, saying, "Hey there." I can tell he's pleased as hell with himself. He leers at me, his mouth curling into a sinister grin, and I try not to scream. If I scream he might hurt me worse than he already has. That's a definite probability—his willingness to hurt me no matter the cost—given that he risked being seen dragging me here.

I recognized his voice. It was familiar beyond a doubt. I've heard it so many times, that I'd known it was him for sure from the moment I woke up. No question. His voice was unmistakable, that tone and cadence. That makes this even more confusing. Why me? Shaking the rags being used to tie my hands and feet to the bed, I look to my right wrist, and I realize it's part of one of my favorite shirts. I gather up whatever courage I have left and ask, "Why? I trusted you. I tried to at least." My voice is full of desperation thinking that he might be able to sympathize with me. It worked sometimes in the movies, so there's always the slim chance.

"That was your first mistake," he says. His voice is chiding, like I was a small child being reprimanded for not sitting still during story time. "Never trust anyone."

My eyes regain focus after I don't know how many minutes, and I can finally fully see him. He's leaning over me, and it makes my frantic heart pound harder with each agonizing second that ticks by. My chest hurts and it pounds faster and faster and faster. *Thump. Thump. Thump.* It's unceasing, especially as his impossibly widened eyes bore into me. His irises are surrounded by tiny red veins and I can't stop staring at them. They're like cracks in porcelain.

The day had started out so well. I went to lunch, and my sandwich was the best one I've ever had. But I say that every time. I'd picked a BLT because I wanted something quick and easy. I washed it down with a long slurp of pop. My friend offered to pay, like always, but I shot her down. "I can pay for my own damn sandwich."

"Just an offer," my friend said, hands up like two white flags.

The memory doesn't make any difference now. Kind of just a nice thing to remember in case I don't make it out of this alive. We all need something like that. Something to cling to during the worst time of your life. So, maybe it makes all the difference in the world.

We both paid and walked out, with a quick hug as she headed back to work and I headed back home. We hopped into Ubers and went on our way. I shouldn't have done that. I should have... I don't know what. Told the Uber driver to speed as fast as possible back to my apartment. I should have sprinted up the stairs and locked the door behind me, pushing a heavy chair up against it. That might have bought me some time, if he truly had planned to capture me.

You always think of stuff like this after the fact, after things are already a lost cause. I hate that, the way your mind completely fails you at the most critical times. You stop paying attention, and everything goes to hell.

I had no idea as my friend pulled away in a silver SUV with their Uber driver who was following me in his own car. The last thing I remember is him waiting at my apartment. I just wasn't paying attention.

Now, an uncomfortable bead of sweat slides down my cheek again. It's so damn hot wherever I am. The AC unit above me isn't humming. Usually in houses like this, they get loud this time of year, trying to keep up with the summer heat. Moisture dampens my underarms, despite having most of my shirt torn off. I feel weirdly embarrassed, sweating so much. This is a vulnerability that he doesn't deserve to see. He doesn't deserve to see my pain, my fear, my discomfort, after doing all of this to me.

My eyes dart around, taking in my surroundings. My vision's slowly coming back in spurts, then it gets blurry again. I can make out unfamiliar old floral wallpaper, no doubt the remnant of the seventies obsession with it as a decorative accent. It's peeling off around the door frame, and I can see a browning wall looking back at me. This house has a voice and it's howling at me to escape as fast as I can.

My nose is irritated by something and I try to identify whatever the smell is. I pick up on a musty stench, like a mixture of damp and age that I hope I'll never smell again in my lifetime. Which might not be very long, but I'm trying to remain hopeful. That's not exactly easy, but I know I need to try.

My worst nightmares were a hell of a lot more pleasant than this, being tied to a creaking bed, with him sitting across the room from me. He was completely upright, his posture rigid, in an olive colored chair, the fabric frayed around the arm rests. The chair is in front of a grimy window, framed by sheer white curtains, just opaque enough to keep out light and keep others from seeing in.

After he approached me, he had the audacity to tell me I shouldn't trust anyone. How is that possible? How is it possible to go through life without trusting a single person? Everyone has at least one friend, or family member to rely on, don't they? I definitely have people that I can trust with my life. Now I'm not sure if I'll ever be able to again, or if I'll even have the opportunity.

I feel a wave of anger coursing through my body, starting from the top of my aching head. He must have struck me at some point. It courses all the way down to my feet, which are still tied to the posts of the bed, the same as my hands are. My face glows hot with rage and I seethe, daring him to not just look at me, but see me, and see what he's done. It might force him to ask himself how someone could do something like this.

Where the hell am I? I've wondered this about a million times at this point. And why am I with *him*? What did he do to me? My mind craves understanding, reason, a basic sense of meaning, anything. But I'm left with nothing.

He goes back to the chair, after the stern warning about trust, and sits there in disarming silence. He's quieter than I've ever seen a person be, watching me, like a hunter watches a deer before firing a fatal shot.

"I couldn't help myself," he says, after a few minutes of staring at me. I hadn't asked him anything. He just wants to hear himself talk, I imagine. "Just one of those impulses."

"One of those impulses?" I say, shaking against the bed posts again. My eyes drop down to my jeans as I feel a chill. Only now, I realize my dark-washed jeans are down around my ankles, as is my underwear. I must have blocked it out entirely. "An impulse is buying a..." My breath is shaky and long sentences are hard to get out. "...buying a plane ticket to Paris. What the—" I open my mouth and let out a guttural yell, tears brimming over my eyelids.

What did he do?

Before I get the chance to gather my thoughts, his face grows dark and he lunges at me, his eyes now inches from mine again.

"Like I said," he says, emphasizing every single word, "I couldn't help myself. And I'm taking this." He dangles a keychain over my head, a corny lucky rabbit's foot I'd gotten from my best friend. He strokes the soft, purple fur against my cheek. I can feel vomit rising in my throat, and I try to choke it back. "Just in case I need to relive this."

Chapter 1

Charlie

September 2015

Phil squats down, his face set in a scowl, and pokes the body with a long stick he picked up on our walk down here. He was prone to doing that, which I hadn't needed to take much time to notice, since he does it each time we're at a scene. I asked him why he did that eventually, and he told me that he'd done it since he was a little boy and he could still hear his dad calling after him. Apparently, his dad would holler, "You're gonna jab yourself in the eye if you fall, and guess what? That's not gonna feel too great." But he did it anyway and, as he was happy to point out to me, never once jabbed himself in the eye.

Phil told me that story over drinks after we solved a case a few months ago and it made me think of my own father, rest him. My dad never minced words if he could help it and his humor was an acquired one to most people. Not to me, though. He always made me laugh and I missed him every day, especially at a scene. Not because of the dead bodies I find and my dad being dead himself, but because he would have known exactly what to do, and would have even told a dry joke to break up the tension. A little uncouth perhaps, but that was his way, and to be fair, people in my line of work could use a little more humor in their lives.

I smile at the memories as I stand behind Phil, watching him examine the body. It was a welcome distraction from the grotesque scene before us. I say nothing, giving him some time to form his own conclusions.

I shiver, even under my jacket. It's a chilly morning for early fall. I've gotten so used to warm September weather the past few years. Damn climate change. The forest is littered with red and orange leaves fallen from the trees above, and now they cover the undersides of our booties. A light fog blurs the surrounding area, clinging to the ground around the body.

The victim is decomposed beyond recognition, and I see Phil suppress a gag. I don't blame him. I'd been to close to a couple hundred crime scenes like this, and this one was especially distressing. If I could guess, she'd probably been in the river for at least a couple months, and her limbs are covered in wet leaves, mud, and other detritus. The ground around the river bed is soaked after rain and our boots squelch through the department-issued shoe covers.

This is Phil's fifth homicide since passing his detective exams four months ago. I know he still struggles with it—the bodies, the circumstances—and I can't fault him. I remember what it was like more than a decade ago when I got my detective badge. Phil tells me that he doesn't understand how people could get used to the smell, putrid and decayed. I say, "You never do. Your senses just learn to adjust better."

Phil gags again but attempts to compose himself, letting out a few slow, deep breaths. He knows we have a job to do, so he pulls on a pair of latex gloves and squats down even lower to examine underneath the corpse's fingernails. After a few minutes, I nudge him in the back, and he almost jumps out of his skin.

"Let's let the techs do their jobs, huh? Plus, I want to set down the coffee I've been holding for you for 30 minutes."

Phil stands up, probably glad to have his nose that much farther from the corpse. He peels off the gloves like they're dripping with poison. "Thanks." He takes a sip out of the warm thermos, and grimaces. The first sip appears to not sit right, so he holds off on a second one.

My dark hair is pulled back in a tight bun, my curls sticking out from the hair tie despite my best efforts, and covered with a hat that has the Chicago flag on the front. The base of my neck itches and I'm dying to let my hair down later at the office.

"You'll get used to it. Soon, it'll be as familiar as the dumpster outside your building."

"That's lovely, Charlie. So full of humanity," he said, one eyebrow cocked.

I shrug. "I've been doing this for fifteen years now. It's hard to see the vics like this, every single time. I always go home sad. Hell, sometimes I cry, and have trouble falling asleep at night. But after a while, you learn to compartmentalize. You get really good at pretending, like it's just another day at the old nine to five." I yawn, and know full well I have bags under my eyes. After inhaling the scent, I take a quick sip of coffee, relishing the feeling of the warm liquid making its way down my throat.

When we got there, a tech had told me that there was no identifying information. No wallet, keys, no phone to search through. The squad's going to have someone comb the river where she was found and back toward where she might have been pushed in. The river is long and leads out into the much larger Chicago River. She'd been found off the path from North Park. Who knew where she might have come from? I need to know answers to questions like that to help solve the case, but there are so many days when I wish I didn't. I'd rather close my eyes and pretend none of this was happening. But someone has to help them.

The perp covered their tracks well, letting her drift away like that, to avoid any footprints or obvious DNA at the scene. The techs hadn't found any fingerprints on the body yet, but the day was just starting. I try to stay optimistic even though I know it wasn't likely prints would show given all the time she had spent in the water.

Phil sips the last dregs of his coffee as we walk back to the car, having gotten over his bout of nausea. Behind us a swarm of crime scene techs descends on the body like flies.

"Hit me with it. Initial impressions?" I ask, and take another long swig of the dark cream-filled brew before it gets too cold.

"Not the work of anyone in the area," Phil says, his voice quavering at first, then growing in confidence. "Like they say, don't shit where you eat. Less likely to be found out."

"You never know. It's not the work of anyone here that we know of *yet*," I say and point my finger at him. "These guys can fly under the radar easily if they're careful. Luckily for us, technology usually catches up."

"Usually?"

"Usually." I click the remote to unlock the car, and Phil gets behind the wheel. I always let him drive so I could take notes about the scene. Sometimes, it's easier than I care to admit to get caught up in my mind and let my brain engulf itself in theories and what ifs. I need to remember as many specifics as I can for my report.

"You coming?" he asks. I pause, staring back at the hiking trail we'd just exited.

When I became a cop, I did it for the usual reasons. The clichés you always hear about. I do it to help people, and make the world a better place. After walking through a scene like this, I find myself wondering how I'm doing in that regard. It's like playing whack-a-mole. There are days when I wish I'd gone into medicine, student debt be damned. Maybe become a nurse, like my mom.

I take one lingering look back at the woods, thinking about the slow movement of the water as it courses through the river. Where had this poor woman come from? How long had she been floating? Who would do something like this?

A monster. Plain and simple. These cases are perfect examples of how cruel humanity can be.

I close my eyes and take a deep breath. "Yeah, coming."

Chapter 2

Dannie

April 2021

The floor catches me hard on my left side as I land with a thud on the wet tile. I kneel before getting up, not wanting a painful repeat.

Rubbing my elbow, I remembered I'd put the small floor mat in the wash, along with some towels. Shit. That was a couple of days ago. Someone had definitely stolen them by now.

Vultures. But, who could blame them? Times weren't always easy trying to make a living in a major city. I know I don't exactly have the cleanest conscience. I'd stolen the odd pair of jeans left behind, and once, a sweater. Let them have my cheap ass towels.

I stand up, and scrutinize myself. Wrists, ankles, back, shins, head, nothing seemed injured. I take a nice, deep breath. I'm not dizzy, my vision seems fine. There aren't any bruises or scrapes to let on that I'd fallen out of the shower like an idiot. Getting injured freaks me out. It has for a long time, and I have a tendency to fall down frequent internet rabbit holes. I sit naked on the closed seat of the toilet and order a new bath mat and some towels on my phone before I forget.

Glad my elbow doesn't hurt too bad, because I have a long day of work ahead. Another photoshoot at some blah, unremarkable house that Ashlin is trying to find a tenant or buyer for. Not the most exciting day in the life of a photographer, but it was my life, and what can you do sometimes?

After wiping my damp hands on a gray towel hanging on the wall, I fumble for a small tarnished silver flask in the bathroom cabinet. It was just a fall, not a car accident, but my mind tells me otherwise. I close my eyes and take a gulp. My throat burns, but I instantly feel more relaxed.

Still wet from the steamy shower, I pat myself with a towel that used to be a hell of a lot fluffier. I know I need to make a trip to the store, but I'm always putting it off, and Jeff Bezos delivers faster than it takes to convince myself to set foot in a home goods store. It involved leaving the house and dealing with the public. I did enough of that at work. Plus, those places always smelled like a sickening amount of lavender, like my grandma's house did when I was growing up.

I yawn and glance at the time on my phone. 7:28. It is way too early considering how late I was up trying to talk my friend Rosa through another dating crisis. Sifting through my black linen hamper of clean laundry just outside of the bathroom that desperately needed folding, I fish out a black fleece sweater and a pair of skinny jeans. As of last week, the weather had finally transitioned from cold to cool. April in Chicago is good for that when it isn't pouring rain, and I love it. One of my favorite things is sipping coffee in front of my small living room window which is currently propped open by a book. The hinges need to be fixed, and that was yet another thing to do that felt like too much. So, broken it stayed. I'll call my landlord eventually.

I trudge to the small kitchen that's tucked into a corner next to my living room. The little amount of cabinet space I have above my stove isn't the best, but I make do with it. The brown wood needs a new finish and the hinges creak, and that reminds me I keep meaning to ask Rosa if she'll help me spruce them up. I take a peek inside.

Unfortunately, I'm out of coffee. And eggs, and anything else that resembles breakfast food. A half empty box of Townhouse crackers, and a jar of peanut butter isn't going to do it. I could always make that trip to a store like I knew I needed to. But on a day like today, it's easier just to head to the diner. It's gorgeous out, and Rosa repeatedly tells me that a daily walk might do some good.

Rosa also says I need to stop drinking so much. I know she just wants to help, but it's not something I don't already know.

I run a comb through my short, cropped hair. The other day I dyed it darker again with some boxed color Rosa brought me from a nearby drug store. It had always been a relatively dark brown, but I liked this new shade of black. Black is kind of my thing, as much as the *they must be goth* stereotype makes me gag.

I brush and floss for a few minutes, throw on a coat and sneakers, and walk out of the door. I lock it behind me, twisting it a few times to double-check. It's been a long time since there's been a break-in in my building. Luckily, I landed in a pretty decent neighborhood considering the crime rates in this fair city. But still, you can never be too careful.

After a short walk down the hall and a flight of stairs, I step out into the glaring sunlight. I hunch over and cover my eyes like a goddamn vampire. After the late night the sun feels like needles piercing my skin. Yet another unsolicited piece of advice from Rosa, that I needed to get out of bed before ten since I'm in my thirties. Barely. Thirty-two doesn't count. I love her to death, but she treats me like her kid. To be fair, sometimes I need it.

I wake up early when I need to, but that isn't always the case since my job's flexible. I often have a few days off in a row, depending on the time of year. On those days, I love lying in bed, not being committed to any schedule, my eyes closed even though I'm awake. Being lost in thought is more comfortable than feeling lost during a conversation.

It's not like I have someone to wake up next to anyway, someone I'm always excited to start the morning with. It can be a lonely life, but it's the one I have for now. I appreciate Rosa's care and the advice, though. She means well, even though she can be more annoying than a summer gnat. Rosa is my best friend regardless of our differences, and her maternal instincts make it more special. She gives me a hell of a lot more advice than my own mom ever did, and I'm more grateful for it than I'm willing to let on. No sense in inflating Rosa's ego. She's pretty enough as it is, and smart, and funny, so her brain doesn't need much help in that area.

Truthfully, Rosa is the only person I can rely on, apart from my other friend Ashlin. By *rely* I mean *please come get me because I'm drunk*. That type of closeness. I don't have many other friends, just tenuous relationships I keep with most of my co-workers. Our conversations boil down to: "Hey. How was your weekend? Yeah, mine was alright. Thanks." Basic water cooler chatter. Something holds me back from going deeper and diving into the murky waters of friendship, from being myself. Being myself hadn't worked out so well for me in the past.

I stroll a few blocks past the famous field and across Addison to one of my favorite spots, Café Flora. It's bustling with the usual breakfast crowd, exhausted moms who need a quick hit of caffeine, and corporate bigwigs who are in such a rush to catch the train that they find the need to yell at waitresses. Depending on the time of year it's also a hot tourist spot. After breakfast they clamor for a photo opportunity outside the stadium, like someone there has a winning lotto ticket to give away. I will never ever understand what's so great about sports, but to each their own.

Flora herself is a firestorm of gray wispy hair, messy apron, and rapid-fire commands. She encounters a lot of unkind people in the restaurant business, and she dishes their attitude right back to them. It might be a smaller place, but the food's the best in the area. Flora kept people coming in regardless of her snarky attitude. She always brushes off the negativity knowing her family comes first and she's got a business to run. Plus, anyone who really knows Flora knows she has a soft heart for those she loves. She has a habit of taking in strays.

With the ding of the bell, Flora looks up at me. She nods, eyes crinkling into a smile, all while handing change back to a customer. It is pure chaos at breakfast time even during the week, and Flora's at the cash register today. No matter how busy she was she always had a smile for me. She was another much needed mother figure in my life. This was one of the first places I came to when I moved to Chicago, and Flora treated me like one of her own, even giving me a family discount. I tried to refuse but, well, it's always hard to say no to Flora, and she didn't appreciate the attempts.

I made my way up to the counter, sat on one of the green stools, and asked for my usual cup of black coffee and a short stack slathered in homemade syrup. In an attempt to be spontaneous I also got a side of bacon, moderately crispy. Might clog my arteries, but it was worth it. The server who usually worked the counter during the week says, "Look at you. Bacon with your pancakes. Wonders never cease. What's next? Creamer in your coffee?"

"Shit no," I said.

Right before I get my coffee a fifty-something year old guy in a suit eyes me up and down, a crease forming between his eyebrows. Affecting the Joker's voice in my mind, I wondered why the hell he was so serious. Under the counter, I clench my fist open and closed, a coping mechanism that stemmed the tide of annoyance from boomer morons. Occasionally.

I was used to the looks by now, and I could hear people's thoughts as if they were in my own head. My short hair, my gender neutral clothes, my old sneakers. I wasn't "dressed the part," as they say. I never was. And I didn't want to be either. I wanted to be me after a lifetime of pretending to be something I wasn't.

The server brings me my order, and I take a long gulp of coffee, even though it's still super hot. My tongue burns but it gives my mind something else to focus on. I can see the silver-haired man staring at me in my periphery. Without giving him the dignity of eye contact, I say, "Is there something you want to say, ask, complain about—What is it? I can take it."

He scoffed with typical indignance at being scolded by a millennial. "Just curious, that's all. No harm meant, ma'am."

Curious. Like I'm an oddity in a circus museum. "I'm non-binary, and I'm into women. Some non-binary people dress feminine or masculine, some don't. It's none of your business." I silently took another sip and waited for it, the same thing that always happened.

"Look, I'm not homophobic. I have a niece who's gay."

And there it is—the good old "I have a friend who's..." excuse. As predictable as any team in this town blowing the playoffs. One thing I hate infinitely more than sports is a misinformed cis-het man. Google can teach you just about anything, but apparently seeking out a little education is too difficult for some people.

He slaps down a couple dollars for a tip, mutters an apology to me, and walks toward the exit. I stay, finishing my cup of coffee and first forkful of gooey pancakes, and sigh.

It's not as if I wasn't used to this by now. Misunderstandings about gender weren't unfamiliar to me. I'd grown up in a conservative area of Wisconsin. Every Sunday my family sat there in church as close to the front as possible, maybe thinking their proximity to the cross gave them an inherent moral value and a golden ticket to the Wonka Factory in the sky.

If I closed my eyes, I could relive it all over again. The sound of my mother's voice, the way it slapped me harder than a strong hand. It was the worst day of my life. Just six years ago, I was Danielle, a twenty-six year old photographer living at home with her parents. Danielle had long brown hair and stormy eyes that often reflected her mood. The part about my eyes is still true, to be fair.

My parents had been at a loss. I acted out constantly and nearly flunked out of college. I had to make up an extra semester to graduate, with the help of Rosa. My parents wanted me to have a *normal* life like theirs: settle down, get married, get in good with the Lord, and pop out a couple of kids.

Eventually, I couldn't take the judgment anymore. The choking criticisms made it hard to breathe, like I was trapped forever in a place that was supposed to be home. My mom and I had it out in the kitchen. As it turns out, she, my dad, and Jesus weren't a fan of my sexuality or gender. So, that was neat.

Heated words were exchanged and that was that. I moved to Chicago soon after that fight, and I haven't spoken to her or my dad since. I don't have any brothers or sisters, since my parents had struggled with infertility. The only correspondence between us were birthday cards from home that I never opened. They surprised me every year, and I wondered if it was a small attempt to make amends, but I refused to open them. It was as if my parents were watching me through a hidden camera, and I wouldn't give them the satisfaction. The cards remained shut in a desk drawer underneath a bottle of Ibuprofen and an extra phone charger.

I look at my camera as I walk past my desk, and I recall how many hard times photography's gotten me through. A lonely adolescence, and a somewhat lonely adulthood. I'm glad I get to do it for a living. I love working in photography, but it could be unstable depending on the time of year. After a few months in the city, I was able to find steady work with a real estate agency in Wrigleyville and felt lucky for that. The agents there helped me find a decent one-bedroom down the road from their office.

Thankful that family drama is all in the past, I choke down the rest of my pancakes. I head up to the counter to pay my bill with a quick smirk and wave at Flora. I could tell Flora had seen the man walk out annoyed, and she gave me a reproachful look all while stifling a giggle. I had what you might call a reputation at Flora's. Of course I defended my gender identity, but sometimes I could be a bit… much. My words, not Flora's. There have been times she's asked people to leave on my account. She let their tab go unpaid as she said, "They're a human being, you piece of garbage!" Chicago was pretty progressive, and always voted blue, but that didn't mean that everyone living there shared the sentiment of equality.

I start the walk back to my apartment. It's still early, so I shove my hands in my pockets and flip up the collar of my jacket. The cool morning air caresses my neck. It makes me smile, and I enjoy the rest of my walk. Periodically I glance at my surroundings, as if I was seeing them for the first time.

I glance at the green and beige behemoth that is Wrigley, and I know that it had been a good decision to leave Wisconsin. Over the past several years I've made Chicago feel like home. I've gotten a decent job and an apartment that wasn't the height of luxury but served its purpose. Occasionally I even feel happy, especially on mornings like today, boomers notwithstanding. Since I moved I laugh a bit more, love the few friends I have, and feel much safer than I did back home.

I make it back into my apartment several minutes later and hang my keys up on the hook like always, right above the mail tray. I feel like I can use another cup of coffee, even though I don't make it nearly as good as they do at Flora's. I look back to make sure the keys are there. If I had a dollar for every time I'd lost them, I'd be living in West Town with a view of spas and overpriced clothing stores.

I kick off my shoes, and they land sort of near the mat that says, "Shoes here, please." I'd gotten it when I first moved in, trying to make the cramped apartment feel homey. The subconscious action ate away at me for a minute and I grunt with displeasure. I let out a big huff and walk back, my fist clenching and unclenching. Goddamn it. Fixing the shoes, I put the balled up socks neatly inside and take a deep breath.

I hate that about myself, the need for control over the simplest things, and it frustrates me to no end. There are days it makes me want to run away and not look back. That's why Wrigleyville is an amazing fit for me. It has the ability to swallow a person whole in a crowd of baseball fanatics and rabid tourists. I feel simultaneously less alone and more alone. People can't see the things about me that I hate the most.

Most mornings, come mid-spring or early summer, I walked through throngs of people snapping pictures and hoping to catch a view of one of the famous players. During baseball season the big red sign set starkly against the green and white of the massive field always had at least a couple dozen people underneath it trying to take a picture. I could blend in, like a childhood game of hide and seek, and be completely myself. Yet I could still keep certain parts of myself hidden if I wanted to. That suits me just fine.

I pull my phone out of my pocket and rattle off a quick text. I'm feeling sentimental from the memories of leaving home, so I message Rosa. We've been best friends since grade school.

How was the date last night? Is Mama going to approve?

After a few minutes, I get a reply.

No, because she's never going to meet him. He was a total dud.

My frown at Rosa's misfortune quickly turns into a smirk. The friendship between us is so easy. I know that Rosa craves the chaos of the local bar scene, and she's kind enough to give me a frequent break from the noise and close proximity with strangers.

Just another reason why we're best friends.

***

I head over to my office. If it could even be called an office. What it is, is a large black desk in my living room, pine painted with black lacquer, with two monitors on top. It has a reasonably comfortable chair that I'd gotten at an estate sale and a surge protector underneath. The desk takes up about a third of the already tight space, but I need it for work. Kind of important since half my job consists of editing pictures and checking emails.

On the corner of the desk near the window is a small succulent that Rosa got me for my last birthday. She told me it might be rewarding to have something to take care of. I groaned at the time, having no intention to take care of it. But I did, and she was right. It does feel satisfying in a strange way. When I need sage, maternal wisdom, I go to Rosa who has spent her whole life going to her own mother. Must feel nice.

For extra pizzazz I had also placed a simple silver framed photo of the two of us from college, repping for UW-Mad with our Bucky Badger shirts. That was before a semi-permanent scowl had taken up residence on my face, when I knew what it was like to be carefree. We had genuine smiles plastered on both of our faces, and Rosa was making a peace sign with her tongue sticking out.

The picture elicits a feeling of joy. I fucking love photography, even casual, unedited snapshots like the one in the frame. I even got a degree in it way back in my early twenties after nearly flunking. But real estate photography can be so dull. When I escaped from Wisconsin redneck hell, I pictured myself traveling to faraway places, taking pictures of exotic beaches with a cocktail nearby. Or a luxurious European city, filled with centuries-old, colorful buildings. Anywhere that was not the Midwest.

Then reality hit. I needed money once I got to Chicago, and the real estate job kind of just fell into place. It was okay for now, and it paid the bills. The routine became comfortable before too long, and now it's just the way life was. I've done three shoots already this week, and I'm craving some solitude.

Right at that moment, Google Chat pings on my left monitor. That's the monitor I reserve for boring admin sort of work: emails, conversations with coworkers, and anything else I don't find stimulating. I sit down and for a minute my eyes grow bright, and my heart leaps. The message is from Ashlin. Okay, sometimes that monitor *is* stimulating.

Ashlin has a way of making me feel things that feel pleasant yet unpleasant, in the best sort of way. She's my other good friend. She works at the agency and is one of the most promising younger agents there according to our boss. Ashlin's kind and good at her job. She's also the most beautiful person in the world. I swoon every time I'm around her, then catch myself and snap back to reality.

Ashlin's chipper, pleasant to a fault, and always has a ridiculous smile plastered on. Not usually my type, but that smile works for me somehow. What appeals to me the most is that I can tell there's more underneath Ashlin's joyful surface, a puzzle missing half the pieces. I just haven't been able to figure out what it is yet.

She's hetero, so there isn't a shot in hell. Ashlin's been seeing the same guy for about three years now. He's kind of a dick. Okay, he's a huge dick. He's a trust fund kid with mommy issues, his hair slick with gel and empty promises. But she acts happy for whatever reason. I'll never understand it, but maybe it was a straight girl thing. Besides, I don't really have room to judge broken people.

When Ashlin introduced him to me, we were at her apartment. She had out a delicately curated cheese and meat board she'd posted about on social media, whatever you call those things. Writing about my life on social media's not my style, and I always feel behind on the latest trends. There was a veggie platter with homemade dip, and a fancy counter top cooler with top shelf mixed cocktails in bottles.

He slithered into the small gathering like a garden snake. It was just me, Ashlin, and Rosa, and the first thing he said to me was, "So, you work with Ashlin. How's business these days?" Code for: *How much money do you make?* People like him were all the same, insecure rich boys whose credit card limits were a metaphor for something else. But I tried to give him the benefit of the doubt for Ashlin's sake, even though he made my skin crawl.

I never stop thinking about Ashlin. At least, I rarely stop thinking about her. She crosses my mind dozens of times a day. Her laugh, her smile, her eyes. There's nothing unlikeable about her, even her annoying little quirks. Her obsession with designer labels, and things like the cheese board, and the chipper tone she tries to take when she's delivering bad news instead of just giving it to you straight. I love all of those things.

Even though she's straight, I'm not in a good place to date anyway. I haven't dated in years, nothing really serious since moving to Chicago. Nobody ever seems to be a good fit for me. I meet someone for drinks and we talk mindlessly for an hour or two, my head resting on my chin in disappointment. Your aunt's latest pyramid scheme? Don't care, but at least there's a small amount of comedic value. Your neighbor's been cheating on his wife? *Super* don't care.

On the days when I'm in desperate need of that sort of companionship, my head gets in the way. I have myself completely convinced that I don't deserve it for whatever reason. My delightful childhood probably hasn't done me any favors there. But at least being single is saving me money on picking up the tab on dates.

I pull myself from my thoughts that have managed to wander away and look back at my computer. The Google Chat message says:

Hey, can you go out to a property on Wayne Ave? It's a long shot, but recent work done/cleaning, and we need some good pics from the best!!! He wants to relist ASAP. It's a rental, and we can't get a freaking tenant in there for some reason. Thanks! You're the coolest! 4761 Wayne. Meet you there. :-)

The excessive punctuation is a bit much at times, but I don't care because she's such a good person. An annoyingly good one actually, to the point where it baffles me. Nobody is this nice. At first, I thought there was a catch, but after six years I haven't found one yet. She's kind to me and took me under her wing right away, a few months after I moved here. Ashlin always hypes me up to the other agents there, helping me get regular work in and out of the agency. I obviously need it, as is evident by the worn second-hand couch behind me that's losing its seam on the bottom. Apart from Rosa, Ashlin is all I need in the friend department right now.

Suddenly I feel a chill crawl up the center of my spine. *Ugh.* 4761. I'd been there before for a shoot a couple years ago, and it wasn't the loveliest place on earth. My mind shoots back to the bad vibes oozing out of the walls, like pus from an open wound. Granted, that was before the cosmetic work the agency had insisted on before a new listing, so I'm curious how it looks now. But I can't forget the dread I felt the first time I was there, like it would be a perfect setting for the latest Jordan Peele movie.

I have to go, and I hate it. Even though I already worked a lot this week, near-daily Flora visits mean I need to do as many shoots as possible, despite the discount. Her pancakes are like a drug, and much better than anything you could find at the local grocery store.

My fingers take a moment to think. Ash is impossible to say no to, but I'm exhausted and I hate that damn place. Finally, I type:

Sure thing. Be there about 10:30 or so.

The three dots of her reply linger for quite some time before she says:

OMG you are the actual best!!! I owe you one. I know it's sort of a strange house.

Yeah, that's one word for it. But money talks as they like to say in old movies, and my bank account is seeing a therapist. I grab my camera and huge bag with lenses and lighting equipment, and start hoofing it back down the stairs.

Wayne Avenue is lined with houses closely set together, mostly modest two-story homes covered in dull siding that could use a powerwash. The front yards are small, and there's barely any room in between to scoot through the fences to the even smaller backyards. Still, it isn't a bad area to live in, and it's close to a bunch of good restaurants. I walk over to Diversey and Lakewood, and sit and wait ten minutes for the 10:15. After the quick bus ride, I get off and start walking to 4761. It's not super far from the stop, and hey, now I can tell Rosa I went for two walks today.

As I approach, my feet drag behind me. I know I need to go to bed at a decent time tonight. Out of nowhere I feel lethargic, my feet glued to the concrete sidewalk. I stop outside of the house and spend a couple of minutes staring up at it. The exterior does look a hell of a lot better, like they'd had a landscaper there and maybe did a paint job on the door and window trim. But something stirred inside of me. Something that felt uncomfortable and dark. It was like standing at the edge of the ocean, watching a storm roll in, ice cold water lapping at my feet. I can hear the claps of thunder in my mind and I close my eyes.

The creep factor is probably because the owner's a recluse and never shows his face at the office. He's never contacted Ashlin even though she's the agent on the listing. On the rare occasions that he contacts the agency it's through our boss. And he does it by email because he lives in an area that has bad reception and he says it's easier for him. I try not to judge anyone on their lack of social skills since I'm shitty at it myself. I'm not exactly winning any popularity contests.

It's a running joke between me and Ashlin, wondering who he is and what he does for a living, why he had this property to begin with and never seemed to be in the area, and why he couldn't get anyone to stay more than six months. We come up with all sorts of scenarios, each one more unlikely than the last. Ashlin's latest was that he was a European businessman who doesn't want to lose the equity, but is far too wrapped up in multiple affairs to stay on top of keeping on top of the property. His poor wife. Her name's Alessandra and she recently found a series of letters from other women, sitting on top of the correspondence from the real estate agency.

I smirk and take out my collapsible tripod, attach the camera, and snap a few pictures of the front of the house, angling it so the midmorning light hits it in the right way. I make my way around the property and do the same in the back, having to leave most of my equipment out front so I can scoot through the narrow passage between this and the neighbor's house. The house casts some weird shadows, but I can always tweak the lighting when I'm doing my editing.

I look at my phone more than once. Where the hell is Ashlin? She's usually super punctual. I need her or another agent there on shoots to let me inside for interior shots, and we try to be as quick as possible, especially when it's an occupied residence. Three dots indicate that Ashlin is typing now.

On my way, I promise. Held up by a slow Uber driver. But I think it was his first day, so it's all good. He's really nice.

She pulls up about five minutes later, waves to the driver, and turns around to smile at me. Like clockwork, I feel an unwanted heat flooding my body, even on a chilly spring morning. It pulses from my head to my toes and lingers in especially unwanted places. That's the last place I need to be thinking about right now. I have to try to shake myself out of it before I get to work, or I won't be able to concentrate and get any good shots.

"Sorry, Dans. That guy got lost, even with his GPS. Poor guy. Anyway, let's go in and get started!" Her tone this time is especially animated, all her sentences like excited exclamations, which is cute in a way that's living rent free in my head.

Ashlin rushes up the front steps rubbing her hands together, about to burst at the seams. "We might actually be able to find a tenant, or convince this guy to sell. I can feel it in my bones," she says. She loves the thrill of taking a disaster and turning it into someplace liveable, and she doesn't hate the praise that comes with it.

"Hey, thanks for getting here so quickly. You rock," I said, my mouth curling up at the corners. Even with my flat affect, Ashlin's face lights up like a sunrise, her rosy pink lips set in a perfect grin.

"Anything for the best photographer *anywhere*." She puts the key in the lockbox, and I roll my eyes. I'm not fucking Ansel Adams, but I'll take it where I can get it.

As soon as we step inside I get the chills again. Jesus, no wonder no one wants to rent this dump. Despite the owner getting enough cosmetic work done to make a tenancy or sale viable, it still isn't exactly warm and cozy. There's just something about it I can't put my finger on.

I set up my tripod and lighting and make my way through the main level, pondering all the possible options for photos. To the left of the entrance is a shoe closet, and to the right is a living room which consists of an old brick fireplace, two dark yellow couches that look like they smell like pee, and an easy chair. There are a few paintings on the back wall. One is a generic one of a sailboat on Lake Michigan, and the other one gives me the fucking willies.

It's a picture of a carousel, the horses in desperate need of a paint job. It's actually a hauntingly well-taken photo. Good use of lighting and halfway decent editing. But I just imagine the music in my head and shiver. Sitting in the corner on the ground between them is a creaky old rocking chair, and if I stare long enough I swear I can see it gently swaying back and forth, as if someone's just stood up.

Ashlin chatters away behind me with multiple polite critiques as I do my thing. They aren't directed toward me, of course. She always lets me work in relative silence while she discusses any recent updates to herself.

"This wall color? I don't know. I know you hate beige walls. It can be a bit outdated but whatever. At least it looks cleaner now." I can hear her typing on her phone. "The trim's a bit of a hack job in the corner there, but maybe the renters won't notice. Please pretty little Jesus, tell me they replaced the carpet upstairs." More typing.

The house doesn't really look too awful from an aesthetic standpoint. If you didn't count the serious Amityville aura. I snatch my stuff and we walk up the stairs. Ashlin scans the carpeted staircase area for any potential issues, finding just a creaky step, but I couldn't care less. I'm too preoccupied with the quickened beating of my heart with every step I take.

Why did I watch scary movies with Rosa a couple of nights ago? I always end up overanalyzing life for a couple of days afterwards.

Take my heavy feet outside of the house earlier for example. I couldn't even walk in without forcing myself to. It's stupid, but the back of my neck is clammy and I wipe at it the second I have a free hand. The sweat is cool and relentless.

There are two small bedrooms upstairs that butt right up next to each other, each one about ten by ten feet, just large enough to hold a bed, small bookshelf and chair, and a closet that Rosa would call distressing. The walls are the same bland beige as on the main level, and the trim's recently been repainted white. There is a single full bathroom located in the hallway with a clawfoot tub and a gray and white checkered patterned shower curtain surrounding it.

When Ashlin, me, and my camera equipment make their way to the last bedroom I peek inside again. Turning to Ashlin I say, "What do you think about the lighting in here?"

"It's not perfect even with your lighting gear, but whatever. A couple of floor lamps go a long way. Here, let me fix the curtains a bit. Maybe some sun will help. It's starting to get a bit cloudy though. Are you okay?"

After a few seconds, I realize I've been staring into space, and she has to repeat what she said. I shake off the feeling and step into the room.

One I do, I scan the area and take a mental inventory of the pictures that could be useful for the listing. The bedspread was ugly as fuck, but renters could just replace it. Lord knows I would. Maybe I can tweak the color a bit in the edit. I'd replace the general ambience here, too, if my editing software would let me. If Rosa was here she'd say we need to toss some sage around. It had all the charm of a stack of bricks. As I adjust my lens and set up the shot the air conditioner kicks up a notch.

"Well, good to know that works fine," Ashlin says and types a bunch of notes on her phone, laser focused while I start to line up a shot.

About a minute after she says that, we look up at the vent on the wall. "The fuck is that rattle?" I ask.

Clank. Clank. Clank. The vent rattles over and over, and we get a little closer, inching slowly toward the bed that sits in front of that wall. Ashlin stays behind me, so near that I can smell her perfume. It's sweet and citrusy and it takes all my strength not to breathe it in.

I turn around and I can tell Ashlin's fighting the impulse to chew on her fingernails. She'd mentioned the other day that she'd just gotten them done and loved how they turned out, so she must be spooked. I look up at the vent, eyebrows furrowed and my mouth set in a pout. There's something inside the vent. I can see a glint of metal from the sun coming in through the open window.

"That's not exactly ideal, is it?" Ashlin says, her voice making a vain attempt at positivity, despite the unsettling situation. "Dans, you're taller. Can you see inside?"

Clank. Clank. Clank.

"You have a quarter in that purse you paid too much for?" I ask, not meaning to be sarcastic. That's just our unspoken conversational rhythm.

"A quarter?"

"Yeah, or a nickel. These vents have Phillips-Head screws. I don't have a screwdriver."

"Oh, right," Ashlin says, and she begins rummaging around in her purse that could have fit three small dogs. "Here you go." She hands me the quarter, and I start to work it into the grooves of the screws.

After a few moments, I have the screws off and I'm pulling off the vent. I yank it clean off and a small cloud of dust blasts into my mouth through a gust from the air conditioner, making me cough. When the cloud settles I say, "Huh." What the hell am I looking at? I mean, I know what they are. But why are they there? My head pounds and I wish I had one of my pills with me.

Ashlin gasps. Like Rosa, she watches way too many horror movies. "What is it?" she asks, her anxiety obvious in her increased tone of voice. Her South Carolina accent comes out even more when she's nervous or upset and it's insanely intoxicating.

"Just some keychains. There's a bunch of them. Weird." In all my years working for the agency, I'd never seen anything like this. I replace the screws on the vent and climb down off the bed. After I wipe my hand on my jeans, I put it on Ashlin's shoulder, letting it linger. "Don't worry. No human remains that I'm aware of. It doesn't smell like rotting flesh."

Ashlin lets out a strained laugh. "That'd be a major turn off, huh? A recent murder investigation? We better skeddadle."

I realize my hand's still on Ashlin's shoulder and yank it away, my face flushing. I put the keychains in my pocket, and as I do I feel my damn head pulse with an impending headache again. The hip underneath the pocket prickles with goosebumps and I move to grab the flask out of my other jacket pocket, but I stop myself. She's staring at me like she can read my mind.

Chapter 3

Rosa

April 2021

"I swear to Jesus," I say under my breath. It is *way* too early in the day for this. He's calling for me like his loafers got chewed up by the dog I don't even have. Not enough caffeine consumed yet, and yoga had been canceled that morning. I sigh and do the sign of the cross, full well knowing what Mama would say. Taking the Lord's name in vain fell just under not having a second helping at family dinners. His voice is grating as he calls me into his office a second time.

Louder, I call out, "Sure thing, be right there."

It's a slow trudge to his office. He is odious, rude, abhorrent, unseemly. I try to think of a lot of adjectives in my head, but my brain's complete mush. Everyone knows someone exactly like him. He's like the villain in a period drama, with a hideous mustache, who's uncouth and out to slander me by any means necessary. When I finally get there my boss is sitting at his mahogany desk, scribbling a quick note with a fancy fountain pen engraved with his name. "Here," he says. He hands me the note. "Get this out, will you?"

I take it from him, suppress an expletive, and say, "Okie dokie, Bill. I'll get right on it." I'm teetering on the brink of secretly looking at a job search site on my lunch break.

"That's my girl." He takes a swig from the whiskey tumbler at his side. It's only 9:30 in the morning, but he was already four or five fingers deep, like he's a modern day Don Draper or something.

My girl, my ass. He says that to everyone. Like I'm somebody special. I roll my eyes, heading back to my desk in a room full of cubicles. It was just far enough from Bill's office to allow for a little gossip. My quiet chats with my work friend, Evan, and my texts to Dannie were what got me through the day. But the distance between the desk and office had been Bill's choice, not mine, no doubt so I wouldn't report on his numerous affairs to his fellow ad agents.

It's a busy day at the office. Assistants furiously typing copy for their supervisors, others lugging around four packs of made-to-order coffees for the higher-ups, and a couple of meetings that can be easily overheard through the glass walls. "This is more effective, and you know it. Red? It's for a spa. It's like you're new here. No one wants to go to a spa with red font on the ad. Blue. Blue is relaxing. Redo it." Evan leaves the meeting room in a huff, locking eyes with me as he passes, as if saying, *Help me.* He's used to taking his fair share of criticism, but that's all part of the gig if you want to work your way up and make the big bucks, as they say.

Evan and I met at work several years ago, and became friends pretty quickly. These days he's busy with his jam-packed dating rotation schedule, trying to find Mr. Right. But every so often, I'm able to weasel my way into a drink or two after work. I've got to hand it to him for trying.

I sit back down, the note from Bill in hand, and open up my email. I CC all the relevant copywriters and BCC Bill. That's how he wanted it done as he told me millions of times. It's one of his favorite dad jokes. "Do it just like this. Down to the letter."

I start with the subject *Urgent,* and then continue to type Bill's message in the body of the email. With each word I type my mind grows more vacant with tedium. I'd rather be taking verbal abuse for my terrible copy and actually be able to use my brain to think of a retort, over the monotony of sending out message after message. I hit send and then I hear my phone vibrate inside one of my drawers.

I'm not technically supposed to use my personal phone unless I'm on my break. I try to keep Dannie on the straight and narrow by setting a good example and playing by the rules, but this is one of my only forms of rebellion—sly texts under my desk. I look around, biting my lip. Bill's still in his office, getting tipsy well before lunch, and the other supervisors are in meetings. It's Friday, and they all have deadlines to meet.

I slide the drawer open and peek at the message. It says:

Are we still on for next weekend? I already canceled my church meeting for Saturday.

I groan. Damn it. I forgot I promised Mama she could come into town and stay with me next weekend to celebrate her fifty-fifth birthday. And canceling a church meeting means business. Church life is like its own separate form of religion for her. Papa died last year of cancer, but I know the visit would be huge—my three sisters, one of whom was married with kids, and my four living aunts and uncles. I do have a huge sectional and a pull-out couch, but there's no way that's going to accommodate more than ten people. I quickly click on a travel deals site, book five rooms, and text Mama back with the details. My reply:

"A hotel room? You didn't need to do that, mija! Thank you. You always take care of your Mama."

That's because I know I have to. It's as deeply ingrained in my DNA as my out of control curls. I'm the oldest and need to be responsible for all these chuckleheads. My younger sister has three kids now, at thirty, and often forgets things like this. She chalks it up to mom brain, and I can't blame her. My sweet nephews—I swear they're sweet—are a handful. My two youngest sisters are still more of the secret clubbing types and aren't nearly as responsible as they ought to be. But the clubbing is really only a secret to Mama. No one has the nerve to tell her.

There goes my next paycheck. Hopefully, my midyear bonus is going to be good. But it's Mama, and I have a hard time saying no. My mind is now in full wander mode, and I jump at the ping of an email reply from Bill.

God meeting. You typed god instead of good. FYI. Otherwise god job.

My eyes narrow, and I reply:

Thanks. Will spell check next time.

This was one of those times I wished I kept a flask in my desk like Dannie, even though I give them shit for it. I go through my inbox and delete a few spam messages, then reply to a catty email from Evan.

Bill is such a dick. Good luck with what's his name tonight. I can't keep track these days.

I smile, and I hear another buzz in my drawer. What now?

It's my cousin, Marco. The texts are fewer and farther between these days unless he needs money. I know what the message would say before I even read it.

Hey, Ro. Can you lend me a couple hundred? I'm behind on rent.

I know exactly why that is, but know I have to reply with caution. He has a tendency to fly off the handle. I ask:

You okay?

Yeah, been worse. Just need a little to get my landlord off my back.

How he hasn't been evicted from that shithole, I have no idea. His boyfriend's no help. Logic tells me I can't save the world. It's the oldest child in me, the classic savior complex. I got my party animal sisters out of trouble with Mama, planned everyone's birthday parties, and attempted to have a social life on top of it. With the family's upcoming visit, I don't really have the mental room for Marco. Despite the internal conflict that causes me, I love him so much and wish I could help.

I would if I could. I just dropped a goddamn fortune on the fam so they can visit for Mama's birthday. Wish you could come. For the money issue- Where's Tony at? And what happened to the new job? The bussing job.

Marco moves through jobs like sick people move through tissues. He ignores my question about Tony.

Late too many times. Been having problems waking up on time.

I look around to make sure Bill's still in his office.

Again? Have you been to the doctor?

Can't do that when I can't even make my rent, can I?

Fair point. I hate doing it. It goes against every fiber of my being, betrays my already heavy conscience, but I type back:

I'm sorry. I really can't. Maybe next paycheck. Or when I get my bonus in a couple months. But listen, you take care of yourself. Please. I love you.

I wait a few minutes but no response. That wasn't totally abnormal. My heart sinks when I think about Marco. We were so close as kids. We'd huddle under the dining room table before dinner when the rest of the family was too chaotic and tell each other jokes. It's difficult to tell yourself that one of the people you love most in the whole world may be beyond help. I put my phone back, close my drawer, and put my head in my hands, kneading them into my forehead.

Eventually I get a reply. It says:

It's okay. Texted a friend. Thanks anyway. Love you too.

I swallow, a large lump forming in my throat. I know what kinds of friends Marco has. I hear the sound of expensive loafers coming out of Bill's office, so I start absentmindedly going through some memos on my desk. Maybe Dannie will know what to do. But Dannie has enough problems as it is.

Chapter 4

Ashlin

April 2021

My short pink manicured nails click and clack across my keyboard, and I blow my hair out of my face with a massive exhale. Email after email has been coming in about potential listings and showings. It's awesome, though. It's the sign of a good season. A lot of our best business is in the month or two before the end of a school year, and it usually lasts until the next one begins.

I'm working at home today, typing on my laptop at my mahogany desk. Well, sort of mahogany. It's really pine, but I paid one of Eric's friends to refinish it for me. I would have asked him, but Eric isn't exactly the manual labor type. Now, it looks like it cost three times what it did. A picture of me and him on a ski vacation last winter in Vail sits next to the computer. We stayed at a gorgeous little chalet, with faux-fur lined blankets, plush couches, and a real wood burning stove—his attempt at apologizing for a recent fight. On the other side of my monitor are flowers from a recent client. A cozy little work space, bookended by something negative and something positive.

Dannie says I should dump his ass, as they put it in their usual acerbic way. But it's so hard to leave something behind that's been a part of you for so long. He's like a bad habit, a drug I don't know how to stop using.

I wrap my sweater tightly around my chest and lean back in my swivel chair. A spring chill bites at my arms, and I regret turning off the heat last night. My last email gives me pause, and I don't know what I'm supposed to say. It's about a nearby property we've tried to sell or find renters for numerous times with no luck. Apparently, the owner did some renovations and wants to relist the property with the new images. It's kind of a running joke between Dannie and me now—the mystery of the Wayne Avenue house. Not that I don't trust them to do it justice with some great pictures, but it's just one of those places that feels like it's meant to stay vacant.

I grab my phone from the side of my keyboard and type out a quick text. I know Dannie will answer quickly if they can. They always do. I chew on my lip and wait for a reply from them. It does come quickly, saying:

Sure thing. Be there about 10:30 or so.

I smile and breathe a sigh of relief that I'll be able to just get this over with, thankful they're always willing to drop anything to help a friend. Not that Dannie has much of a social life. Really it's just me and Rosa. Still, Dannie means so freaking much to me. The thing I value the most in life is loyalty, having someone I can count on. I type back:

OMG you are the actual best!!! I owe you one. I know it's sort of a strange house.

I groan, silently berating myself for the triple exclamation point as soon as I send it. It had been an unconscious choice and a common one for me. It feels cringey, but it kind of aligns with the personality I've worked so hard to cultivate. Happy go lucky, perfect life, perfect apartment. Perfect everything, even though that seemed to be lacking lately.

Eric steps out of the bedroom behind me and squeezes my shoulders. I jump a bit, despite hearing him approaching. I'm still pretty pissed about last night, and my nerves are a little frayed. "Busy day today?" he asks, his voice measured and calm.

I shrug and stand up, grabbing my phone. "Not too bad. I'm about to head out on a shoot with Dans, and then might have a few things to clear up at the office. How about you?" I put my hands on his shoulders and draw my body closer to his. My heart yearns to mend things. To not have things always feel like they're my fault, and to not be the one to screw things up. I look into his bright blue eyes, but he just looks at the ground. They were one of the things that drew me to him in the first place, and lately he shows them to me less and less.

Our fight last night hadn't been completely abnormal. I'm choosing to chalk it up to a case of having been together for three years now and moving in together recently. Really I know it's a series of small cracks, growing into a larger spiderweb I can't clear out.

Eric shrugs. "Gotta head in. Dinner tonight?"

"Not sure. I need to see how work goes, and if anything comes up."

He nods and heads out the door, a messenger bag slung over his shoulder. It feels cold, the lack of goodbye, and I pull my sweater even tighter. This isn't how I want things to be, and I don't know what I did wrong. I watch him leave, holding back tears. When is it going to be the last time he walks out of that door?

***

Dannie effortlessly unscrews the vent cover from the wall. I'm good with interior design. I can make anything look pretty, or at least pretty enough. But this sort of thing is *so* not in my wheelhouse. Dannie makes stuff like this look easy. I usually outsource handiwork to them or one of Eric's friends.

"Huh," Dannie says. Their face is stoic as usual as if a broad smile would be their cause of death if they ever allowed one, and their brow furrows a little in confusion. They're never one to show many emotions, at least not on the outside, but I've been learning to read them. Even after several years I can still see that they aren't ready to completely open up. They barely talk about their childhood or teen years. All I know is that Dannie left home after coming out as nonbinary, but I want to know more.

I want to know everything about the person I've become so close to. Isn't that what friendship's all about?

I gasp and bring my hand to my chest as Dannie's hand comes out of the vent. This is just like that documentary on Netflix, *Finding a Killer*. It's a show I just started watching the other day while Eric was out, about how detectives use forensic evidence to solve decades-old mysteries. I love mysteries and the thrill you get when you pull your blanket up a little higher to cover the bottom half of your face. But they also terrify me, which I guess is a mystery in and of itself.

It's a TV show. Don't be stupid. "What is it?"

"Just a few keychains. There's a bunch of them. Weird." Dannie puts them in their pocket. They put the vent cover back on and get down off of the bed. They put their hand on my shoulder and say, "Don't worry. No human remains that I'm aware of. It doesn't smell like rotting flesh."

I try to laugh, but it comes out sounding forced. "That'd be a major turn off, huh? A recent murder investigation? We better skedaddle."

When we get outside a few minutes later I turn to Dannie and say, "I hope there's not a shitstorm with Cheri about this."

"Why would there be?" It sounds confrontational, but I know it isn't.

"We can't take things from houses, Dans. It's like real estate agent 101." This isn't meant to be confrontational either, but I'm worried it sounds that way, so I add a nervous laugh. Apart from me getting in trouble at work, this could get Dannie in trouble as well.

Dannie tells me it's going to be alright. They're always great at that. After a bit more conversation I say, "Meet up tonight?" The last damn thing I want to do after this morning is go home to a cranky boyfriend who's always spoiling for another fight these days.

"Yeah, I'll text you."

We split off, Dannie likely heading back to the bus and to their apartment to edit, and me to the office to answer some emails and do some thinking. I wait a few minutes on the sidewalk pacing around and shivering and wishing I'd brought a jacket. This time, luckily, the Uber driver shows up a little quicker. I normally don't care that much about how speedy they are. They're all just trying to do their jobs and make rent, same as me. But right now, I want to get as far away from this house as possible.

As I ride back to the office I wonder, am I doing the right thing? Besides the fact that I should have offered to ride share with Dannie, there's the moral and professional issue.

Normally I pride myself on being a good person, on doing the right thing and being kind. It was a sharp contrast from my childhood. My mom's a total narcissist and expected us to be extensions of her. I was always on my A game as a kid. I had to be, or Mom would call me out on it. Even if this was the wrong move, Dannie already took the keychains, and we can't undo that. We can always return the keychains, but the situation bugs the hell out of me. I've never taken things from a house before.

I bring up my fingers and massage the bridge of my nose. It's Dannie getting into my head. I kind of have a tendency toward short-lived friendships. Most of them last less than a year or so. I always try to be positive, the optimistic one, and that was apparently a turn off to people in my age group, despite what my mom led me to believe as a child. I have a few casual friends I hang out with when I'm super lonely, but normally my couch, and Dannie, were enough to satisfy that need. And Eric. I almost left him out, there.

I have no idea when I became so aware of my insecurities. Maybe I've always known and just pushed them to the back of my mind. I overthink things, and that leads to a *ruminate-click through Netflix-ruminate more* spiral. It feels impossible to make new friends in your thirties, but Dannie always gives me a chance to be myself. Well, most of myself. I wasn't ready to share the rest. They listen to me vent about work, Eric, my mom, anything that comes up, and I would do anything to keep things that way.

I can't go getting them in trouble and losing them. That would be like losing everything.

I hop out of the car with a thank you to the driver and walk into the office, thoughts still on Dannie. Sitting down at my desk, I take off my heels and kick them under my desk, with a little more vigor than usual. They might be a designer brand, but my feet are killing me.

Dannie may put on a closed book act, but I can feel how tight we are in the little things. A well-timed pat on the shoulder. A sly smile. How they call me *Ash* and *sugar plum*. They always go out of their way to help me with things at work, even after a busy week. Dannie even helped me move around a bunch of heavy furniture when I got a new couch.

Dannie had made a big production out of it, rubbing their hands together and huffing out a loud exhale. It was hilarious. "Ash, I'm not gonna lie. I don't like the odds here. We have no hope at all of making this look well-staged." They winked and squatted down to lift their end of the gigantic leather ottoman, while I struggled with mine.

I can be honest with myself. I see these subtle flirtations. They're happening more often as the years pass. It's innocent enough, nothing inappropriate. And it fits somehow, almost like a corner puzzle piece of our friendship. It's possible Dannie wishes there could be more, and I hope that doesn't make them sad, if so. That would devastate me, but I'm not sure what else to do.

Sometimes if I'm sitting alone at night with nothing else to occupy my thoughts, it sits there and gathers in the empty recesses of my mind. Instead of finding the flirting off-putting, it feels as comfortable as the couch Dannie helped me put together. That in and of itself is the part that feels strange.

Chapter 5

Charlie

January 2016

I could have smelled it from a mile away, the scent of death mingling with that of the wildlife and mucky water winding its way through the river. It haunts the area, and I know I'll go home smelling like it, same as I always do. There's no amount of body wash, detergent, or scent beads in the world that can rid me of it, because I carry it in my heart even more than I do on my clothes.

The surrounding area is clustered with police, crime scene personnel, and a handful of rubberneckers. That's not unusual. Murders especially seemed to draw out a bunch of true crime obsessed lurkers. I can't blame them. Curiosity about death is what leads a lot of people like me into working in homicide in the first place.

I wonder if any other local jurisdictions have come across anything as horrifying as this. As soon as I get back, I ought to put out some feelers. Other cops tend to keep things pretty close to the chest about this sort of thing, but you would think a decomposed body of yet *another* young woman would be enough to get them to share some info. Especially with such similar circumstances to the body we found several months ago.

This poor angel washed up a couple of days prior, I'm guessing, and based on the amount of insect and wildlife damage, that wasn't when she died. Decomp looks like probably about a month or two's worth, but I need to wait to see what the medical examiner says.

My heart cries for these young women, and I try to not let my eyes do the same. I wear a flat expression so that other cops feel better. It's hard to do your job when you're busy dealing with a lead detective who's in tears.

According to one of our crime scene techs I talked to by the yellow tape, there's nothing apart from the strangulation marks and petechial hemorrhaging in both eyes. So far, no hint of DNA, but the tech had only been there an hour or so at the time. No identification, or wallet. Her clothes show normal wear and tear given her current condition.

The lack of personal items is odd. It's the same as the last case. Who leaves the house without at least their phone these days? People in their twenties and thirties use their phones like another appendage. I can also remember many, many teenage lectures from my dad about remembering my license when I went out. "You never know what kind of creeps are out there. And you can't always trust the other drivers." Always the optimist. I smile, but then I start to wonder what kind of families were missing these women, and I instantly deflate like a balloon.

I approach the body and squat down, careful to not let my booties knock around any potential evidence. I think for a couple of minutes, my eyes scanning for any obvious clues. "Anything stand out?" I ask, already predicting the answer.

This tech just joined the squad and is eager to prove himself. Police precincts can be a bit like dick measuring contests, and new hires get a little insecure. He clears his throat, "Okay, well, nothing yet, ma'am. Just the signs of strangulation. It sucks, doesn't it? When these bastards cover their tracks so well. I hope the ME comes back with better news. Just about done with my pictures and then I'm gonna head back to the lab to take a look at a couple of skin samples."

I nod, knowing he's doing the best he can. "Good work, Aaron. Keep it up."

He grins. "Thanks, boss."

I return the grin. "I'm not your boss. Just trying to solve a mystery, same as you." I head back to the group of officers clustered next to their squad cars, Phil holding court with his newfound confidence. It's good to see him finding his footing.

They stop talking as soon as I get there, and Phil holds his hand up to me as if to say, *Chill.* I know for damn certain what the uniforms all thought. It's not too hard to guess. I'm a black female cop who passed them all up for a promotion. What they seem to forget is that the promotion involved scoring well on exams and being able to run more than a tenth of a mile without getting winded. They're supposed to stay in shape, too, but it's easier for them to slack the lower they are on the food chain.

"Make sure the scene stays blocked off, and keep the press away. Until we know what we're dealing with, the last thing we need is the media fucking this all up for us. You know how they are." I spot a couple of vans approaching in the distance. "Vultures. Let's head back, you two." I indicate a couple of the cops. "Phil, I want to talk this over with you."

"Sure, Charlie," one officer says, his eyes on the media vans.

"Detective Carlson," I say and get into my car. I pull away from the scene, thinking about how young the woman looked, maybe just ten years younger than me. So young, so much potential. What could she have been if she'd had the chance?

I get an email several hours later, after the team finishes dragging the river around where the body was found. They found a set of keys. No fingerprints thanks to all the time in the water, but there was a broken chain dangling from them. Like someone had ripped off a key or a keychain.

Chapter 6

Dannie

"We can't take things from houses, Dans. It's like real estate agent 101." Ashlin pleads, a pout turning her usual smile into a frown. But then she laughs. She probably thinks that came across as harsh.

It's a perfectly normal reaction under the circumstances. I know Ashlin loves her job, and I love that she loves it. It is pretty damn weird, though. Keychains in a vent aren't something you see every day, and my introspective nature is real fucking curious about it. She thinks Cheri's going to be pissed.

"Listen," I say, able to read Ashlin's inner monologue. "I get that it's weird. But if we leave them, the clanking is a possible problem for potential buyers. I mean, maybe they could fix it. 'Oh hey, look, we found some keychains.' Fix, bam. But I already took them."

"We've known each other for a few years now. This sounds awful, but you know how much I rely on the commission. I know money isn't everything, but…" Ashlin clasps her hands together, as if in prayer.

I sigh. "... But it kind of is, I know." Ashlin's trying to save for a nicer apartment. She could sell most of her purses and shoes and buy a McMansion, but whatever. I always told myself that I wouldn't connect with more people than I need to here, since people had a history of getting to know me and rejecting me without a second thought. I can still hear my mother's voice, and see her cheeks flush as her voice got louder and louder. "Well, what am I supposed to call you then? You tell me you're not a girl, but you're not a boy? It's one or the other, isn't it?"

But Ashlin always ropes me in like a goddamn bull and hasn't disappointed me yet, not even once. She bats her expertly mascaraed eyelashes, once again clasping her hands together. She smiles in a goofy way, trying to make me laugh. I can always tell.

Her effort almost works, and with another sigh I say, "Well, sugar plum, we have a few options here. One, put them back. We relist, get some showings, and people are put off by the rattle. Not necessarily a deal breaker. Easily fixed. But you know how some people are. Two, we tell the agency we snooped. They told us to just take pictures and bounce since you have a showing in a bit…"

Now, it's Ashlin's turn to sigh. "Or we say nothing, blah blah blah, and no one will ever know—except maybe the owner who left them there for some weird reason."

"Maybe he won't even know. He's not Mr. Social Butterfly. We hardly know anything about him, and don't know what he will or won't do. He's had this property for years now, and you've never even met him. None of us have."

Ashlin nods. "You're right."

"Maybe he did put them there, forgot, and now it's no big deal. Maybe he shows up at closing, and we say, 'Hey we found your shit,' and give them back." I shrug. "You worry too much."

I put my hand on Ashlin's shoulder, meaning to comfort her. She can get worked up so easily. My skin feels like I'm holding it over a lit burner, and I relish the pain. It hurts to not be able to touch her in the ways that I want to. I stupidly let myself wish, for a fleeting second, that Ashlin didn't have a boyfriend, especially not a shit bag like Eric. Not like it would matter. I don't want to date anyone at the moment. Really. I don't. At least, that's the lie I tell myself.

Ashlin looks up at me, her jade green eyes full of appreciation. "You know, you're right. Not likely anyone would know anyway. You put the vent back on. No harm, no foul. Thanks. You always know what to say. You owe me, though."

My eyebrow cocks up, and I can't help but laugh. "Oh yeah?"

"Meet up tonight?"

"Yeah, I'll text you."

I know I should ask Ashlin to hang out on my nights out with Rosa more often, but the thought of mixing Ashlin with copious amounts of alcohol always feels deadly. One of these days I'm going to get too drunk and ask her to come home with me. My stomach fills with those damn proverbial butterflies, and I can't tell what they mean. Is it guilt? Excitement? Anxiety? It's hard to tell when my brain is a minefield of stupid feelings that don't make sense half of the time.

***

I step back into my apartment, placing my shoes neatly on the mat. Keys go where they go, mail goes where it goes. It made me feel a little calmer and I tried not to question it when things made me calmer. I let out a huge exhale and head over to my work station. I plop the camera bag and equipment down gently in the corner next to my desk and plug the camera into the computer. Once the pictures are uploaded, I get to work.

After several years in the business, and a long history of photography, the editing process is easier than luring Rosa out on half-price drink nights. I upload them to the editing software, and it's simple enough from there. Time consuming, sure, but I enjoy the routine. Routines are comforting to me. They're predictable. Safe.

The major issues in any project tend to be lighting and color correction. Occasionally I need to make the exterior shots look more vibrant. Bluer sky, better sunset, etc. Whatever it takes to add enough visual appeal without lying to potential buyers.

As I go through the dozens of pictures I took, my thoughts wander back to the keychains. What the fuck is that about? The house itself is just creepy in general. My grandma told me once that sometimes you just get a feeling about something. Not that we're on speaking terms anymore, but it's always stuck with me. Feelings are often the most telling experience we can have.

I feel goosebumps on my hand as I click through all the different lighting options. The prickle creeps up my arm like a vine and winds its way to my shoulder.

Suddenly, it's around my neck and I can't breathe. I gasp for air and can't seem to get any.

I slide my chair away from my desk—stopping my work on brightening up an abhorrently decorated room—and take a few, slow deep breaths. In and out. In and out. Rosa taught me that for when my anxiety sets in. She'd learned about box breathing and a whole other slew of things from a book she read when her cousin, Marco, was in a bad place. Which kind of happens a lot these days. I can relate to that.

Rosa has been such a fucking gift to me over the years. She was the first person to encourage me to live my truth out loud, which was scary as hell at first. But she was there each step of the way holding my hand, often literally.

Rosa grew up in a very large, *very* loud family. She has three sisters and an extended family that could fill an entire apartment, if you count cousins, cousins once removed, and all the other branches of her family tree. When I go home to visit for Thanksgiving every year, which started during my years at UW-Mad, her family welcomes me. It's one of the only happy memories I have from my adolescence, that first year at her family's house.

Rosa's aunt had hugged me and caught me up on all the gossip, even though I couldn't have cared less. Her younger sister dragged me from person to person telling them about how well I was doing in school. It made me feel awkward. I don't enjoy being put on display. But in a way it did feel good being treated like a guest of honor, which I always was there, as long as I helped stir the mashed potatoes and clean up afterwards. To this day, it's the best example of family I've ever seen. The days I spend there each year are always happy ones.

In one of those weird synchronistic moments, my phone rings and it's Rosa. The ringtone's some damn hip-hop song that she loves. She relished in changing the ringtone on my phone that plays when she calls. It mutilates my ears but, for whatever reason, I've never had the heart to change it.

I answer, and Rosa's insistent voice is on the other end. "Long day so far, D. Post-work drinks? Please? I'll get the first round."

"Bill being a dick again?"

"Do you have to ask? No, you don't. He is being the biggest dick ever, as per usual. But since I am a teeny tiny hair's length from a promotion I have to put on my happy *Yes Sir* face. It's exhausting, and I hate him. So, six o'clock? Usual place?"

Not that Rosa has to tell me about putting on a brave face. Rosa knows I understand. "Sure. Only…"

I can hear Rosa smirking. That's how long we've been friends. I can psychically hear Rosa's facial expressions. "What, love? You have a hot date afterwards? Did you scowl someone into sexual desire?"

"Ha, *no*. It's just that I sort of owe Ashlin a favor now. And Ashlin wants to go out with us, because we're obviously the two funnest people on the planet." Silence from Rosa, so I continue, "And I kind of implied that that would be alright."

More silence, despite another audible smirk. "Mmhmm. You owe her a favor? One that involves cocktails, then you know, things get wild, you invite her back to your place… That type of thing?"

I roll my eyes. "Jesus, not that big of a favor. I mean, I—Dude, no. She's doing me a work favor, and batted her goddamn eyelashes and I couldn't say no. She can be fun. She *is* fun. You know that."

"She's got the spirit of a Yorkie, but she's nice enough. Why not?"

"Thanks, Rosa. She was super cool about something today, and I'd feel bad saying no." And also, there's the huge secret that could get us in trouble, and creeps me out more by the second, that I now share with Ashlin. And I want to keep Ashlin as happy as possible.

"Mmhmm. Just keep your little paws to yourself. I don't want to play third wheel. And I'm gonna need to know more about this favor."

"Third wheel. As if. She's got Eric, who, thank Christ, is *not* invited." I lower my eyes, ignoring Rosa's last comment about the favor.

"Thank Christ, indeed. Sure, whatever. Tell her six sharp. My ass cannot wait to get my margarita on."

"Thanks, Rosa. See you." I hang up, and open my desk drawer. I don't even have to look. My fingers can grasp the small metal flask from memory.

I've been drinking for as long as I can remember, even before the massive fight with my mom that made me leave Wisconsin for good.

I'd chopped all my hair off, stopped going by Danielle, and changed my pronouns. My parents were livid, of course. It went beyond the scope of their already limited imagination that their daughter wasn't *she*, but *they*. If it wasn't a part of the Sunday sermon, it didn't exist at all.

I remember standing frozen in my parents' kitchen that night, my stomach roiling at being referred to as Danielle. Again. "It's not as simple as a boy or a girl. There are a lot of things in between that you don't understand. And call me Dannie. That's my fucking name now."

The vein in my mom's forehead had pulsed. "For crap's sake, can you watch your mouth? And I named you. I was there. After 40 hours of labor, no less. I wrote it on your birth certificate. Danielle Northrop. Baby Girl. I don't know any Dannie, or any genderless babies for that matter."

"Maybe you don't know me at all, Dannie or otherwise. Maybe you don't deserve to."

Even after several years the pain hasn't eased. I take a long swig from the flask, and I realize I need to hit the liquor store within the next day or two. I put it back and reach around until my fingers find a small bag, take it out, and drop a single orange pill into my hand. Another stop I'd have to make soon.

I swallow it dry. One day, I'll find another way to deal with my anxiety and all this other bullshit, but shrinks give me the creeps. As does meditation, affirmations, and those morning yoga classes Rosa goes to before work. I'm not exactly a natural remedy sort of person. Unless you count the seldom casual encounter with a stranger at a bar, and those were very seldom these days.

After the vodka and Xanax sets in, I finish the pictures, the sweeping video of the recently remodeled kitchen, and email it all to Ashlin. On Google Chat, I type:

Sent pics and a video. Let me know if I need to make changes. And 6pm sharp at The Hole In The Wall. Rosa's having a shit day, and says to be on time.

My fingers hover over the keyboard. I wince and add a smiley face emoji. Ashlin likes that sort of thing, even though I'm not exactly an emoji person by any stretch of the imagination.

Minutes later, the chat pings.

OMG, I'm so excited. *Party hat celebration emoji* I'll be there!!!

I smirk and head into my bathroom. The evening is getting to be a little more interesting. I picture how Ashlin might look later when we meet at the bar. I'm a person with pretty simple tastes. I don't picture her in a tightly fitted black dress, sky high heels, and hair done for Jesus. I picture her the way she looked this morning, which was casual by Ashlin's standards. She's stunning no matter what she wears, but it's still a facade.

An attempt at informality that always makes me curious. What does the real Ashlin look like underneath?

Now I'm here like an idiot in front of my mirror, briefly questioning my current outfit. What does it matter? It's not the real me anyway.

Chapter 7

Rosa

April 2021

They're all losers. Well, maybe not losers. That's a little harsh. But they definitely aren't my type. I put on quite the act at bars, flirting with anyone with a penis. That's just for shits and giggles, though. I try to keep high standards for myself when it comes to actual relationships. Not just because it makes Mama happy. Or my overbearing tías. It's because my ex was such a shit bag, and it taught me that I deserve way more.

My ex, Andy, and I dated for a couple years during college and a couple years after, off and on. It started out well enough, and the sex had been great, but I eventually started to notice a lot of changes in him. He got more withdrawn, more secretive. He was always texting people, and going out to meet them late at night when he thought I was asleep. I thought he was cheating, but he'd come back so fucked up that I knew he was using.

Then Marco came back from Afghanistan, depressed and unable to cope with the emotions that come with leaving active duty behind. Unfortunately, Marco coming back led to Marco meeting Andy for the first time, and well… Andy is no longer a part of my life. I made that quite clear to him several years ago.

I look to see if there are any new messages. There are a few from guys I'd swiped right on recently, and one from a guy who wants a second date. He wrote:

Hey, just seeing if I got your number wrong. I haven't heard back. Hit me up!

Hit me up. Jesus. Like he's a speed bag at the gym. In the dating scene that phrase is always code for, *Let's have sex*. Gross. *Pass*.

I pat myself on the back for not replying. I could definitely use the sex, but not the things that came with an awkward one night stand and a guy I didn't vibe with. I also hate superficial flattery. I roll my eyes and check to see the matches the app assumes I want to see.

I swipe left about ten or eleven times. No one is even remotely interesting. Every guy on here lately is a walking cliché. "Looking for Mrs. Right," says the guy in a white t-shirt and jeans. "I love my dog," says the one with the huge German shepherd on a leash. "Busy guy looking for a little fun," says the guy in a perfectly tailored suit looking at who knows what in the distance. Probably looking at his personal banker. I can tell by the smile.

Again, maybe I'm being unnecessarily cynical. I'm just tired of dates that lead nowhere except sex that was only good for *them*. Dannie always ribs me about it, but I desperately want someone I can bring home to introduce to Mama, my crazy trio of sisters, and the rest of the family, who are all ready to offer my hand in marriage to anyone at this point. Even though I constantly remind them that while I love a good Regency romance, this isn't the 1800s.

Sometimes it's exhausting to be the reliable one. The oldest to a sister who got married young, and to two sisters who could hardly keep steady jobs. I'm the one people depend on. There are times when that's a good feeling, but more often it feels pretty damn lonely. But that's life. We're all alone in our aloneness, and we're never showing people who we really are.

I can see my wedding day in my head. Yeah, I want to get there on my own terms, without Mama's help, but I do want to get married. I close my eyes, and I can see the perfect night as if I was standing right there. Mama would expect nothing less. It would be the biggest wedding the town has ever seen no matter how much it strained their budget. I envision light purple orchids strung across the reception hall and the twinkle of fairy lights above the dance floor.

I'd dance with the love of my life of course, our cheeks pressed against each other's, my arms around his neck. Afterwards, music would pulse through the speakers as hundreds of people lost themselves in the rhythm, drinks flowing like Niagara Falls. And Marco would be there, clean and happy.

All that would have to wait. Right now, I've got more important things going on. Reliability striking again, I dial up Marco. After a few rings, he answers. "How are you?" I ask. "Any job leads?"

"I've been better, but I might be able to get a job in a factory by my place. Tony's got an in there."

I scoff, rolling my eyes. "Tony's got an in. He has an in everywhere, and you know what that usually leads to."

"It's been almost a week since I used, Ro. I swear. I'm going to try harder this time. I even went to NA a few nights ago."

"Have you been keeping up with your sponsor? This shit's been going on for years. And listen, I get it. Things have been really, really hard since you came back. But I'm worried, primo."

"I am, too," he says. "But what am I supposed to do? I don't have insurance. Can't even keep a job. I lose track of time too easily, and I got in another fight with a coworker."

"Christ. Again? Listen, I will pay for you to see someone. Anyone. Anyone other than fucking Tony. He's not good for you."

"Remember how you can't help me with rent this month?" I cringe. That's right. I did say that. "And who *is* good for me? I'm not even good for me. I'm not good for anyone."

"Don't talk like that. You never know who you might meet if you give it half a chance."

"And who am I gonna introduce him to? My homophobic Mama? It's like the elephant in the room, Ro. And it always will be." His voice breaks. It does that when he's struggling not to use.

"You can introduce him to me. Or Dannie. There's always someone to help, whenever you need it."

"Using is the only thing that makes it stop. Maybe I'll beat it one day, but right now it's going to meetings and just trying my hardest to get out of bed in the morning."

I choke back tears. I would give anything to smash his pills and the people he gets them from. I would take a goddamn hammer and obliterate them into dust. And Dannie's pills, at that. I want to save everyone I love. That good old savior complex again, probably not made any better by all the times I'd been too busy with work to take my dad to his chemo appointments.

"Well, please. Keep trying. Keep going to NA. And text your sponsor. Promise?"

Marco takes a deep breath. "I'll try, Ro. Promise."

We hang up and I rest my head on my knees, staring off into space. His promises are a dime a dozen. Now I need to get out of the car and walk into the bar. I know I said six o'clock sharp, and it was 6:02.

Chapter 8

Ashlin

April 2021

I sit curled up on my soft yellow window seat, resting my head against the glass. It's my favorite place in the apartment, leaning back against the gray pillows, my legs pulled up to my chest. It had been a long morning, and I'm glad the work day wasn't filled with too much else after that besides a showing. I'd practically thrown my heels across the room with relief when I got home. I'd texted Dannie back:

OMG, I'm so excited. *Party hat celebration emoji* I'll be there!!!

It reeks of desperation, and I know it. It's typical for me to seem a little bit too excited about things, like a compulsion. *Enthusiasm makes friends.* I can hear my mom's voice in my head, and that's the last thing I need. Despite how much my mom irritates me, it wasn't a total lie. Enthusiasm isn't always a bad thing, and I could use a fun night out.

Things have been so awful with Eric lately. Our recent fight was volcanic, and I could still feel the burn of the magma. I'd come home a bit later than he expected to lukewarm take-out and questions about where I'd been.

"Where were you?" His face was flushed and his eyes intense.

"I had to wrap up a couple extra things at work. I didn't know you got dinner. I'm sorry."

"Yeah? You're always sorry," he said, before going into the bedroom for the rest of the night.

Escaping the negative energy that fills the apartment these days is just what I need.

I don't know if Rosa likes me all that much, but it's alright. Rosa tries, for Dannie's sake I assume. Rosa and Dannie have the kind of friendship where they trust each other's judgment when it comes to people.

The text to Dannie still bugs me. It was so nerdy and I wish I could go back and delete it, but they'd already seen it. I'm terrible at being real and genuine in front of others without sounding like a drunken sorority girl. Dannie has more than once compared me to a yappy dog. Rosa has, too. It's harmless teasing and it makes Dannie smile. But it also makes me wonder if I'm going about things all wrong.

There have been a ton of showings recently, and I'm a little burned out. Eric and I went on a real date a few weeks ago. He'd been nice enough, pulling out the chair for me, and doing all the other things that society had conditioned me to expect. The conversation had been alright, pleasant and easy, but there wasn't any spark anymore. After the date, I spent the night feeling restless, and I couldn't understand when things got so messed up. I want to feel restless in a good way, in an *I can't stop thinking about them* kind of way. It's been a long time since I felt that way about Eric.

When we first met there was passion and easy conversation and laughter and all the normal emotions that come with a new relationship. But lately things are starting to show some wear and tear, and I honestly don't know how much longer I can go on like this.

I rest my forehead on top of my knees. I used to love dating around, and I secretly thought about reactivating Tinder, just to see what happened. It had been fun and, more importantly, made me feel like *I* was fun. It seems like years ago that I craved the feeling of catching the eye of all the men at the bar, and spending the night singling one out to flirt with. Sometimes it resulted in a date, sometimes not, but it was fun all the same.

I miss feeling that way, special to someone. The only people who make me feel special are my friends.

Of course, if I go back on Tinder, Eric's going to find out somehow. He has a way of doing that, sneaking around. I sigh. Let him find out. Can't make things worse than they already are.

I take out my phone and click the Tinder icon. The old Ashlin, who wasn't nearly as self aware about my insecurities as I was now, would swipe right and just see what happened. But I'm tired of feeling like I'm just wasting time. I want to find something that feels authentic. Something that makes me feel cozy inside. I don't want to spend a whole insignificant lifetime waiting to feel happy, but it's starting to feel inevitable. Eric is who I have, who mom approves of, and I'm just stuck. I quickly close the app and delete it. Maybe it is better if he doesn't know.

I put my phone down and make my way into the bathroom to get ready for my night out with Dannie and Rosa. As always, I scrutinize my outfit. I'd picked black skinny jeans, and an emerald tank top layered with a cream-colored button up cardigan. It's flattering I guess, but it feels like yet another layer I was desperate for someone to peel off.

Who am I trying to impress? I guess I could always meet the love of my life there. Who knows? But I scoffed at the idea. Does that even exist?

Eric walks in the front door. Great. He says, "Hey," setting his leather loafers on the mat and hanging his keys on the hook. His tone's clipped, and he huffs before I even have time to respond.

"Hey," I say back, continuing to inspect myself in the mirror. What did I do this time? Is he still mad about me being fifteen minutes late for dinner?

"Going somewhere?" He leans against the bathroom door frame, arms crossed and eyes narrowed.

"Yeah, I'm going out with Dannie and Rosa. Meeting at a bar. I might be out late so you don't need to wait up if you don't want to."

He sighs. "I texted you earlier, remember? We were going to try to watch a movie without fighting. Try something different. Maybe even kiss. Wild, I know."

That's typical Eric, trying to make me feel like I'm crazy for not throwing myself at him constantly. I wish I would have left months ago, but for some reason, I just can't. It's like I'm physically stuck and my feet can't move. My mom would tell me to stay, and I can't shake that. That's how deeply the childhood claws are stuck in. When he says stuff like that, it's like I'm not allowed to feel any other way. "I don't want to try something different, Eric. I'm tired."

"Not too tired to go out."

"I didn't say I was physically tired."

He mutters something under his breath, and without turning around I hear his feet thudding into our room, his footfall so heavy that our downstairs neighbors can probably hear it. He slams the door behind him.

My eyes widen in annoyance and I touch my tongue to the inside of my cheek. I'm sick of it, but I don't know what to do. I can leave, but where would that get me? Lonelier than I already am? I touch up my waves from the morning with my curling iron and apply some fresh makeup. It's only a girls' night—so to speak—but I want to look nice.

***

I had a blast that night. It felt amazing to be out of the confines of my apartment which was starting to feel more like a prison. I'd laughed, leaned in close to listen to Rosa's salacious office gossip about her friends there. Evan was hilarious, and the few times I'd met him, I always made it a point to get to know him more. Maybe I would at some point. Apparently he snuck into Bill's office, and changed his word processor to autocorrect *the* to *asshole*. Bill needs more password protection on his computer from the sound of it.

I caught a few brief glances from Dannie that made me smile. I went up to get another drink when the server was slammed, and I'd look back. Why, I couldn't tell you. But they were looking at me, and sheepishly looked away when I caught them, randomly inspecting their fingernails, as if it wasn't obvious.

It was the best night I'd had in a long time. Rosa and I even hit the dance floor during a few pop songs, laughing our asses off. Dannie watched from the table, comfortable as always being the onlooker.

I usually call Eric to let him know when I'm leaving somewhere late at night to tell him I'm on my way home. I don't feel like it this time. It's just going to lead to another argument. I know him all too well. "Oh, so good of you to tell me. Appreciate it," he'd say. I'm tired of his unpredictable tides of passive aggression and straight out cruelty.

Damn, I'm so glad I moved to Chicago. If I hadn't ditched South Carolina, I never would have met Dannie. Dannie came in for an interview at the agency about six years ago. They're technically a freelance photographer, but they wanted an in at a local agency to keep steady work. I was relatively new to the agency at the time myself, so I didn't have any part in hiring them. But I still remember Dannie's casual wave and wink as they came and left. I find myself thinking about it often, and it's like the feeling of a tight hug.

Dannie's been safe from day one. They're funnier than they realize, and sweeter, too. I always walk away from them desperate for one more moment, which is rare in a friend. I wish Eric made me feel the same way.

Chapter 9

Charlie

May 2016

A third body lies washed up on a riverbed, rotting from months of decomposition, the early summer bugs buzzing around. I swat them away as I kneel down. I want to be surprised by scenes like this, the especially ghoulish ones, but I no longer am. Not sure what that says about me, or about the city I live in.

This time they found a wallet. Stephanie Aspen, local Chicago resident. Thirty-one years old. Lives in a nearby neighborhood. Why is he taking them so close to home? I just assume it's a man at this point. Not many serial murderers are women, and they rarely kill other women.

Stephanie was slender, slightly taller than average, and had the remnants of long red hair. I picture how beautiful she must have been in life. Hair draped over her shoulder, laughing at a friend's joke like she had nothing but a lifetime ahead of her. I find myself stroking the strands of hair and thinking about how fucked up the world is. My dad would have said, "The world might be a messed up place, but good people like you can make it better."

Can I? My eyes are brimming with tears at the question, and I wipe them away with my sleeve.

Around Stephanie's neck is a diamond pendant, the metal beginning to tarnish. Her finger still holds an expensive-looking sapphire ring, even though the finger had begun to lose flesh. Nothing appears to be missing, except her phone. And there's also the predictable lack of a link to the other victims that we can see so far. Doesn't seem like they have any connection at all.

Another river drag leads us to the keys and wallet. Only a house key remains, or what looks like one. No broken off key chains. But there's also no car key, or mailbox key, or key for work, or anything else. Just a house key. Sure, a lot of people in the city don't own a car. But they usually have more than one key, and a lot of times they have gym fobs, or a bus pass holder.

Hopefully, he's wising up. Not like I want him to be getting smarter, but in my experience, the perps get smarter because they start to realize they're making mistakes. That realization sometimes makes them more insecure and frantic, which leads to more mistakes. Might not happen with this one but who knows?

Phil comes up behind me, and says, "Just a house key." I can practically hear the bags under his eyes as he takes a heavy swig of coffee. I stand up and he hands me one, the iced latte he knows I prefer as the Chicago weather starts to warm up. "Extra shot of espresso."

"You're a gem, you know that? You're right about the key. Wanna do the notification, or do you want me to go?"

"I'll do it," Phil says. "You stay until the brass gets here." I glare at him and he holds his hands up. "I had to call them. You know how it goes. There's three now, and an emerging pattern and signature. Clear MO. The chief's trying to avoid the Feds getting involved, but the Bureau's chomping at the bit."

"Yeah, I know. Sorry. I just hate the idea of turning over months of hard work to people who don't even know them."

"To be fair, we don't know them either. Or, we didn't."

"I do. I know these women. Hell, I could have been one. I might not have ever met one, but I can *see* them. Not trying to mansplain being a woman, but you know."

Phil nods. "Sure, I get that. But the Feds can bring in a new perspective. A fresh set of eyes never hurt anything. And you know the chief's gonna fight for us to keep as much control as possible."

I take a drink of my latte before the ice melts. "I know. I know. The job's made me a bit of a control freak, I guess. Especially this case. I don't want a bunch of men coming in here with a half-assed attempt at justice for women. Present company excluded." I watch the crime scene techs buzz around like flies, their arrival more imminent each time a body washes up. They know they need to be faster, more precise, better. They need to help catch whoever's doing this. Us detectives might make more money, but often the crime scene techs are the key to solving the case.

Our chief, Mike, saunters over, eyes roaming over the scene around us. He'd risen in the ranks not for the paycheck, or the power, but because he'd grown weary of crime scenes and looking into the lifeless eyes that came with them. He avoids looking at Stephanie herself and turns to me instead. "Phil said there was only one key. So I'm assuming a stolen keychain of some kind. No one has only one key."

"I assume so, if she had one," I say. "But why? I don't get it. He could have taken her necklace or ring, but he takes a keychain? Probably cost less than $5, like most of them. He could have stolen one of the other keys, but again, why? To get into her mail? Her address is an apartment building. What kind of mail is the average civilian getting? Too young for social security checks."

"I'm not sure, but the Feds are on their way."

I huff. "Let me guess, they want us to step back."

"No, they're fine with a collaborative effort for now," Mike says, voice soft and reassuring.

Phil's eyes dart back and forth between me and Mike, and he takes nervous sips of his coffee. He and I both know that the word *collaborative* means condescension and imposition. Phil looks at me and says, "Let's get back, get a file together, and add the new vic to our board. Try to look like we have our shit together before they get here."

I nod, and we head off. This is starting to feel like one of those cases that we might never solve.

Chapter 10

Dannie

April 2021

The music at The Hole in the Wall pulses in my ears, punk music that's about a decade older than I am. It's your typical bar, complete with pub-style metal tables, a few booths, and a long bar counter. The counter is lined by chrome stools with cracked leather tops and has bottles stacked to the ceiling behind the bartenders. The bottles themselves range from bottom to top shelf, literally and otherwise.

Rosa and I walk toward a newly vacated table, still covered with napkins and empty glasses. You have to take what you can get most nights at a place like this. We sit down and Rosa hangs her jacket on the back of her stool, scanning the bar for Ashlin. I keep mine on. I'm anxious she's not going to show, and I glance at my phone. Ashlin seemed excited at the time, but she might have butted heads with Eric about it. I can always tell, even when Ashlin's too shy to bring it up.

"I said six o'clock, my love," Rosa says to me.

I roll my eyes. "What she sometimes lacks in punctuality, she makes up for in charm. And it's only ten after." My tone is dry after the long ass day. "How was the rest of work?"

Rosa shrugs. "Oh you know, hopeless. Dull. Soul sucking. The usual. *But*, Bill did say he appreciated me sending an email to a client quickly. That's the nicest thing he's ever said. To anyone, I think. His wife's a lucky gal. How was your day?"

I shrug, too. "Went to a property with Ashlin. Snapped some pics—" I stop, wondering if I should tell Rosa about what happened. I've trusted Rosa with much more in the past, including keeping her mouth shut about my crush on Ashlin. Or whatever it is I feel. "Found some mysterious keychains in a vent—" I cover my mouth right as it comes out. Fuck.

As I say it, Rosa looks at me, eyebrows bobbing up, and a server comes to our table. "Hey, guys, sorry. I'll have the busser clean this in a min. What can I get you?"

Rosa perks up and waggles her fingers at the server. He's young, blonde, and probably ten years younger than us. Of course, he smiles back at her. They always do. "Watermelon margarita, please. Blended. Salt rim. Feel free to go a bit heavy on the tequila. Dan?" she asks, looking at me.

"Vodka tonic, neat. Feel free to go incredibly light on the tonic."

Rosa rolls her eyes. "So predictable." To the server, she says, "Thanks, dollface," with a wink.

He winks back, cheeks flushing, and walks off to get our drinks. A busser comes right after and cleans off the table with a nod that says: *I'm super busy, but here's the bare minimum.*

I blink a few times and say, "Alright, what's the secret, Rosa? How did you come by endless amounts of allure?"

She flicks a crumbled up paper straw wrapper at me that the busser had left behind. "I actually make an effort. Give it a try sometime."

As Rosa finishes the sentence, a telltale hint of flowery perfume and the click clack of heels appears behind us. I turn around and draw in a quick breath that I hope isn't noticeable. I cast my eyes downward after I see that Ashlin has changed into curve-hugging skinny jeans, and a shirt the same shade as her eyes. Don't get sucked in, Dannie. Ashlin's eyes have a tendency to be dangerous.

"Hey, Ash," I say. "Just us best pals tonight."

Rosa waggles her fingers again, this time also doing so with her expertly threaded eyebrows.

"Of course! It's been a hot minute, hasn't it? How are you, Rosa?"

"Peachy. How are you? How's the real estate game?"

Ashlin beams and sits down. "Amazing. Dans and I just looked at a place today. The pictures came out great, by the way," she adds, conspiratorially, as if Rosa doesn't know what real estate photos look like and it's our little secret.

I hesitate, trying to not let my internal wincing show on my face. I know I should tell Ashlin that I accidentally told Rosa about the thing we decided we wouldn't tell anyone about. Or, at least, I'd started to tell Rosa. So, I do my best to keep the conversation steered away from the keychains. "Yeah, we got it relisted, and it shouldn't be too long before we get a few showings. Ash did a nice job managing the whole thing."

Ashlin's face flushes at the compliment. Jesus, I can never help myself, can I? "Stop. All I did was take notes and write the copy on the listing. You were my hero there."

I stare down at my drink, just dropped off by Hot Blondie, willing my face not to smile, blush, or give any indication that there are about a million butterflies in my stomach. I hate the cliché, but I don't know how else to describe the way she makes me feel. Ashlin orders a fruity drink after the server sees her and sprints back to the table.

"It was nothing," I say. "You're easy to work with. Rosa's the one with the shit job."

"First of all, it's not a shit job. I've got a place to live, in a good neighborhood. Second, it's my boss that's shit. Not the job itself. As long as I pretend like I enjoy it, the day goes by pretty fast. Usually. Is that sad?"

"Very," Ashlin says and takes a long chug of her flashy pink drink the server ran back with.

After a beat, Rosa bursts into laughter. "Man, you really undersell how funny she is."

This is nice, having a pleasant conversation that doesn't center around real estate mysteries that Rosa would be convinced are a premise for a true crime documentary. That's one thing Ashlin and Rosa had in common. As long as I keep the chit-chat flowing and Ashlin doesn't find out I told Rosa about the keychains, the night should be a good one.

As if on cue, Rosa says, after ordering another margarita, "So, what's up with the keychains you found?"

Ashlin gives me a look that could have easily shredded a designer handbag to pieces. "The *what* about the what now?" she asks, eyes wide with a hurt surprise.

I take a long drink and say, "Okay, look. I know we decided we weren't going to tell anyone, but it just came out. Rosa's my best friend, and I trust her more than anyone. Plus, she always has random, stupid advice that ends up being helpful."

"Gee, thanks?" Rosa says.

"You know what I mean." Eyes focused on Ashlin, I say, "Maybe she can help. She won't say anything, I promise." I shoot daggers at Rosa.

Rosa throws her hands up. "Promise. With pinkies. And sugar on top. And in the name of the Father, the Son, and the house of Gucci and all that."

Ashlin rolls her eyes. "Fine. But no one else. *Promise?*"

I try not to smile. I'd do anything for Ashlin, despite feeling a little relieved I told Rosa. She's a good person to have in your corner. "Course. No one else."

Rosa clears her throat and takes a chug of her margarita. "Alright, now that we've exchanged pleasantries, and discussed the rules about the keychains and shit, let's talk about how creepy that is. Finding them in a vent. Yuck. It's like the bodies at Gacy's house. One vote for creepy," she says, raising a finger. "And the rest of the jury?"

"It's nothing like the bodies at Gacy's house," I mutter.

Ashlin gulps. "The house was super, super creepy. So, I vote yes. Maybe. But it's probably nothing, and I really don't want to get in trouble. I'm, like, two or three good commissions from a better apartment." She looks at me, green eyes dripping with worry. I know what getting a different apartment could mean for her. I've brought it up numerous times, but she swears it's just about the space.

"Another obvious talking point," Rosa says, "is because it's so creepy don't forget about our signal. Remember in college when we'd go out to bars to try to pick people up. Do you remember what we said?"

"You are massively overreacting."

"Tell me what it is, Dan."

Annoyed, I say, "We said we'd never go to bars alone, and always text each other where we were afterwards, even if we felt safe."

I get the hint. Even if the keychains mean nothing, I've still been struggling with my moods lately and have a tendency to put myself in what Rosa, or any sane person, would call *not the best situations*. Might not be a bad idea to do regular *What are you up to?* check-ins.

"It's not a woman's world. Or…" she waves her hand up and down at me, "Sorry, love, you know what I mean. We're unsafe. Always. And we need to stick together. Now that we've agreed on how creepy this house is, try not to go back there if you don't have to. You never know when some psycho could just pop up out of the fucking ether." My eye roll is probably visible to people back home in lovely Wisconsin.

Ashlin sticks up her finger. "Might be kind of hard to avoid since it's part of the job. I'm going to have to do showings and all that. Plus, even though it might seem spooky, I'm sure it's nothing." She looks at me and her voice cracks. Our eyes connect for a minute longer than I'm comfortable with, and when she looks away she takes a sip of her drink.

Rosa says, "Okay, whatever. But it made Dannie feel uncomfortable. I can tell. They're not as good at hiding shit as they think they are." Ashlin gives a quick nod, and Rosa continues. "If you go back, don't go alone. At least make sure another agent or whoever is there. Got it? Text each other. Text me. We'll be each others' wing people. Hopefully, Dannie will do a better job at it than they do at bars."

I give Rosa a pointed look, and then look at Ashlin. "It's nothing. Try not to worry. Rosa's just being Rosa." My words feel hollow, though. Could this really be something that goes beyond a few keychains? Is all this crap necessary? Even if it isn't, the thought of leaving Ashlin unsafe in any way makes me sick to my stomach.

"I'm not gonna leave you hanging, Ash. Promise."

Ashlin gives me a smile that falters a bit. "Okay, fine, no going alone. Please just promise me, Dans. You're both starting to freak me out."

What's with these keychains? Why do they make me so uneasy, when they're something that seems so innocuous? But I'll do the check-ins if I have to. I'll do anything to keep Ashlin from getting freaked out.

***

I sit up, gasping, shorter for breath than I remembered being in ages. I bring a hand to my neck and my heart pounds in my chest. I claw at it, try to make it come loose from my chest so it can stop its incessant throbbing.

After a couple minutes, I rest my head against the headboard and close my eyes. My skin's glossed in a thick sheen of sweat, like I'd been for a jog. I wipe away a bead that's trickling down my forehead. My heart jumps again, and it takes a few minutes for me to steady it.

I bring a hand to my chest and take slow breaths in and out. A glance at the clock told me it was the middle of the night. It wasn't the first time this dream had broken a decent night's sleep. I can usually remember most of it afterwards. This time, once I calm down, a brief laugh escapes my lips, glad it's over. I take a drink from my flask and shove it back in the nightstand drawer.

Why does the dream make me so goddamn panicky?

The details were always mostly the same. My hand slowly grazing hers, our fingers briefly intertwined. The hand holding makes me feel at peace, her soft thumb rubbing the back of my hand. Her green eyes glimmer with light from the morning sunshine.

There are crumpled linen sheets, dark purple, like the ones on my bed in real life. The dream feels so real to me. A different hand with short, bitten nails slowly making its way up a silky smooth arm until it reaches a twist of blonde hair, messy from the night before. I caress it, and whisper into her ear.

Not unpleasant in the least. But then came the horrible part, the part that always made me feel like I was losing my mind.

No matter how often the dream comes, it's still a bit muddled. Hands grazing my neck, applying pressure. They weren't the same soft hands that I'd held just minutes before. They were rougher, like sandpaper, rubbing up against my throat as they squeezed and squeezed. In the dream I wheeze, feeling unable to breathe.

That part confuses me a lot. It wasn't normally part of my fantasies, the choking, and it always left me feeling… *off.* And the rougher dream hands obviously belong to a man based on the way they felt, although I try not to generalize like that. I hate the way the hands feel, and even after I wake up, I dig into my throat to get them off.

It's a frightening feeling I can't read. A feeling that lingers long after I wake up. If it's just a bad dream then why do the frightening sensations creep into reality?

I definitely have an issue with anxiety. Not that I've had it treated. It's an easy conclusion I came to on my own. Mostly, I'm just terrified to confront it. You don't have to have a medical degree to see it. My need for control and order outweighs my desire for help and change. Plus there are the dreams. The self-medicating. The panic. Something is definitely *wrong*, especially in light of these recurring nightmares, and I'm terrified to find out the reason behind my anxiety, my panic, and the looks I get from people when I feel it.

The choking scares the hell out of me. Is my brain trying to remember something I've subconsciously blocked out? I have these dreams often. Would a shrink tell me that all dreams have hidden meanings? Like how the color white means purity or something, probably. And black symbolizes darkness.

I don't really believe in that sort of thing too much, but I do think that dreams might be trying to tell a person *something*. I'm always choked by someone in the dream. Had I been attacked and forgotten? Can anyone even forget something like that? That sounds insane, and there's no way I'm ever going to say that out loud to anyone.

Better to just remember the positive shit. Rosa always tells me to try to find the silver lining. That feels damn near impossible. A shiver runs up my spine and I bite my lip. Jesus Christ, even the positive shit isn't helpful to think about right now. These dreams are becoming problematic.

***

A few hours later, I stretch my arms over my head and go into the bathroom to do all the usual morning sort of things. I don't have any work to do today, so I log on to my computer and do some googling about the keychains. This is so stupid. Yeah, there's always the possibility they're connected to an unsolved case or something, but it's not very likely.

My head hurts and my chest grows a little tight like it was being squeezed by the same hands from my dream. I shouldn't be doing this. I should throw the damn things in the trash somewhere and forget about them. All this is doing is making my anxiety worse.

But a little investigating never hurt anyone. I open up the browser and type *Missing keychains, missing people.*

I just assume *missing* for some reason. Jesus, I hope they're missing people, or they were missing and eventually found. Not dead.

Why am I jumping to something criminal?

I can always call Rosa, but she already cautioned me against doing stuff like this. Google rabbit holes give me palpitations, which I'm well aware of, but it's a compulsion I haven't found a way to stop. My heart pounds as the results page pops up. I feel my armpits dampen as I click the first link. It says, *Four women missing- no phones, wallets, or keys left behind.*

The article looks like it's from a reputable source, a national news station that wasn't completely overrun by conservative ideology. The opening paragraph says:

> **Police in Chicago continue to investigate the case of a missing woman- Melissa Henrike. She has been missing from the Chicago area since 2015. After an initial search of her residence, the police were unable to find her phone, wallet, or keys. This is all the information the police have released to the public.**

I close my eyes and rest my forehead on my hand. Cheri's going to be pissed if the owner notices the keychains are missing and brings it up. But again, he's some dude that doesn't live nearby, and has such poor reception that he's never able to call or text. He says it's easier to email. He'd inherited the house, and didn't want to put down roots in Wrigleyville and do too much grunt work. Blah blah blah. So what are the odds he'd know?

I lift my head up and keep reading. The article goes on to talk about Melissa's life, including a quote from her sister. I can picture her sister so vividly in my mind. I don't have one, but it makes me think of Rosa's family, and it makes me think about how I would feel if it was Rosa. The sister's presumably in tears during the interview, talking about what a wonderful person Melissa is, and how her family and friends will never stop looking for her.

My throat closes momentarily and I gulp. How fucking terrible. I can't picture the reality of not knowing, or the despair the family must feel. I hadn't been sad leaving my family behind, necessarily, but from time to time, I wondered what life would have been like if things were different. If my parents were more accepting. I wonder if they ever feel the longing that families of missing people feel.

This might not even relate to the keychains found. It just says *keys*. Even if there is a keychain missing, it's a common enough object. Just about everyone I know has one, but the hairs on the back of my neck stand up all the same. There 's always the infinitesimal chance it is connected, and that eats away at me. What if I can help bring closure to a grieving family?

Catastrophizing. I'd seen a therapist only once after my move to Chicago and that was what they had called what I was doing. Turning the simplest thing into something massive. Like dropping your coffee and thinking that you're an idiot who's always going to screw things up, and now you're going to drop something else that will probably kill you.

It makes no sense, really. But the therapist said it was common in people with anxiety, to make the worst out of things. She suggested medication—the prescription kind, with a controlled dosage—and more frequent sessions, but I declined. I'm almost afraid to get better. To see what the real me looks like without the bullshit. So now, all I'm left with is a flask, street pills, and a poor sense of self.

I don't know what I'd do without Rosa. She always has helpful advice, whether or not I choose to follow it. She was raised in a much healthier family dynamic. Well, they had family dinners, anyway. Marco might be a mess, and they definitely take advantage of how nice Rosa is. But she at least has a mother who cares, and checks in regularly to see how she's doing. She checks in with me every so often, too.

I know I shouldn't be googling the keychains. They're just keychains. We're not talking about a knife covered in blood. In my head I can see the slow bright red drip falling down onto my living room floor. Goddamn it. There goes my stupid imagination again.

I close the browser tab and go lie down on my couch. After fluffing my purple pillow and wrapping a gray blanket around myself like a cocoon, I attempt to get some more sleep. After about an hour of tossing and turning, and my mind swirling in a billion directions, I open up a text chain with Marco.

Can you swing by? I'm almost out.

Chapter 11

Rosa

April 2021

The dishes stack higher and higher in the sink as more people bring theirs over. My sister, Lillian, chases her three boys around while shouting instructions at her husband, Adam. Ana and Maria sit clacking away on their phones, likely texting each other about the cringey way Adam's trying to help Lillian. The family loves him but he wasn't quite as… I'm not sure, but he wasn't *something*.

I glance over at them, Mama holding court on the couch and flipping between the myriad of TV show options on Netflix. Adam wasn't quite as crazy, probably. My aunts are currently bickering about who the latest Furry actually is on that singing show they watch. Dannie stands next to me, rag in hand.

"Dude, your mom's chicken is on a whole other level."

"Everything about that woman is on a whole other level," I say, lowering my voice. I have a dishwasher but it's small, and already full from all the dishes and utensils used to cook dinner. So I enlisted Dannie's help in hand-washing and drying the rest. Mostly, it gives us a chance to gossip under our breaths.

"What's with Lillian and Adam?" Dannie says, between their teeth. "I thought she was trying to stop being such a control freak."

"She comes from a long line of them, love. Thank God, it seems to be skipping me. Well, not really. But it most certainly skipped Tweedle Dee and Tweedle Dum over there." I indicate my two texting sisters with a wet fork. "They can't even control keeping their cars filled with gas. Have you heard from Marco recently?"

Dannie swallows, and I suppress a sigh. "Did you text him? Seriously? Give me your phone."

"I thought the controlling gene skipped over you. Oh, wait, *not really.*"

I lift up a pair of salad tongs and wave it in Dannie's face, glancing toward the living room. The family's now lulled into silence by the latest season of The Bachelor. Looking back at Dannie I say, "Tell me you didn't."

Dannie swallows again. "You don't get it, Rosa."

"Tell me what's not to get. My best friend needs to get off the pills they buy from my cousin who needs to get off the pills. It's super basic. He was clean for like a week."

"He didn't seem like he'd been using when he came over, if it helps."

I roll my eyes and start scrubbing another plate. "Just stop. Please. I love both of you, but I can't save either of you. It's bad enough with Tía being antigay. No offense, but the only reason you're welcome is because you aren't blood." I instantly regret saying it when a look of hurt fills Dannie's eyes. Talk about Marco sets me on edge.

Turning to my family, I say, "Alright, fam. You all have an early start tomorrow and it's getting late."

Mama turns off the TV with a huff. "That's young person code for *Leave so I can talk about you to my friend.*" She rounds up the others, and one by one they come into the kitchen to hug and kiss me, their *I love you*s and *Call you soon*s palpable.

Mama comes over to Dannie and wraps them in a long hug. "I love you, corazón. Be good to yourself. You look tired. And way too skinny."

It makes me happier than I could describe, the way the family embraced them. I shouldn't have made that comment about the reason they accept Dannie. It might not even be true. Marco's family strife was probably just compounded by the fact that he had a drug problem and bled the family dry financially before they cut him off. I grew up super conservatively, hence the tension with Marco, but Dannie was just another kid to them. It doesn't matter what Dannie's pronouns are or who they date. They're family. I smile as a tear rolls down Dannie's cheek, but my heart tugs at me, wishing Marco was here, too.

Dannie says, "I'll do what I can, Mama. Your chicken helps." They hug again, and the large brood starts to walk out the door.

"Bye, Mama," I call out. "Text me tomorrow when you get home." I close the door behind them, lock it, and make a beeline for the wine glasses. I'd made a point not to clean mine and Dannie's. "One more?"

Dannie shrugs. "Sure, why not?"

I pour more pink colored liquid into our glasses. "I'm sorry. I shouldn't have said it. But it's true. They really do love you, but it's not the same with you as it is with Marco. They gave birth to someone they can't understand, and they stopped trying a long time ago. Plus, he's asked them for money for his shit one too many times."

"I know, Rosa. Forget about it."

I raise my glass and then they raise theirs into the air. "To family, mama's chicken, chaos, friendship, and *not* texting Marco anymore."

Dannie rolls her eyes and drains her glass. "I'll try. I promise I will."

I knew I wasn't going to make progress. At least I'd told them how I felt. "Let's change the subject then. How are things between Ashlin and Prince Eric lately? She didn't say shit about him the other night. Seems like it's been that way for a while."

"There's tension, but she hasn't said why. She kind of keeps that stuff to herself, like she's embarrassed. We usually just talk about other stuff, after she brushes off my attempts to convince her to leave him."

"Like what?" My eyes agape with fake sensationalism, and I take another sip of my wine.

"You know, friend stuff, work stuff, TV show stuff. Just never gets around to Eric if she can avoid it. He's an asshole anyway, and I'd rather not talk about him. I always end up saying something mean. I don't know how she stands him."

"He's hot, for one. And he's flush with cash. But yeah. Our beloved Prince Eric is a complete asshole."

"Ashlin's not like that. At least, not really. It's an act. Their relationship is one of those things, and now it's been a few years, and they're *together*. Ashlin's biggest fear is being alone. She hasn't said that or anything. I can just tell. So what's she supposed to do?"

"I guess she could lean on the shoulder of a good friend who happens to be a good listener, and kind, and beautiful, and only occasionally buzzed on vodka and pills." I drape my arm around Dannie's shoulders. "Who knows? Maybe one day she'll wake up and realize that your charm and enthusiasm for life are too irresistible to pass up."

"What about my vagina?"

"Vagina, shmagina. It's all the same."

"Is it?" Dannie asks with a cocked eyebrow.

"Fine, whatever. I'm just saying, don't write it off as a total loss. We all know they're going to break up eventually, and you'll be there for her because that's the kind of person you are."

"I'm the kind of person who's possibly going to get her in trouble at work by stealing keychains and not staying quiet about it with you. Super great friend."

"It was some keychains. Do I think the whole 'hiding them in a vent' thing is super unsettling? Yeah. Do I think the before pictures of that house deserve a documentary on ID? Yeah. But you didn't do anything maliciously. You've always been curious. You grabbed them, and now it's done." I shrug and go to put both of our glasses in the sink.

"I guess." After a weighty pause that could've knocked me over, Dannie adds, "I've been having weird dreams. And they're getting worse since we found the keychains. It's like my mind has seen the keychains before somehow. Or is trying to give me a message. Ugh, this sounds like something Ashlin would be frantically googling right now." They attempt a smile. "All that wine hit hard, and I haven't been sleeping well. I'm gonna head out."

I take Dannie's face in my hands and kiss them on the forehead. "Fine," I say, hands still on Dannie's cheeks. "But please, don't text Marco anymore. He's trying to stay clean, and deals with a lot of drama from Tony. Think about that therapist I told you about. It helped Marco, for a little while at least, before Dicknose Tony. Really think about it. Take care, love."

Dannie leaves, and when I lock the door, I think about the night. The laughter, the bickering, the wine, the periodic troubling looks on Dannie's face, the smiling... and the absence of Marco. I can't decide whether I want to smile or cry.

Chapter 12

Ashlin

April 2021

W*e're unsafe. Always. And we need to stick together. I'm not gonna leave you hanging, Ash. Promise.*

I'm not going to lie to myself. I'm worried about the keychains. First of all, what are they all about? It could have a perfectly innocent explanation. The harmless prank of a teenager trying to mess with their parents. Or some delusional tenant who hid things in random places. So who knows how long they've been there?

But wouldn't another renter have complained about the rattle? No one had mentioned anything to me or Cheri or anyone at the agency that I'm aware of. It would've been important to know before I made the listing the first time.

It's just super weird, and I'm not about to get fired for something like this. Being rude to clients on a regular basis, I'd understand. Not showing up to work, sure. Things like that were unprofessional, and it would make complete sense for me to be reprimanded for that. But for something that I could easily clear up by asking a few questions? Not worth it.

Am I going to have the guts to ask the questions, though? My thoughts return to Dannie, but then I realize Eric's talking to me.

"Are you listening? What was the last word I said?" His voice is jarring, like a foghorn in the middle of a harbor.

I turn to face Eric. "I'm sorry. I got lost in thought. What were you saying?"

"I was trying to tell you about my meeting at work tomorrow. How I might get offered a promotion." His blue eyes bore into mine and linger a moment too long.

I inch away from him a bit, and say, "I'm sorry. It's just been crazy lately, and I have a lot on my mind."

"Like what? Something more important going on in your world? You can tell me."

My eyes flash back at him. "Tell you *what*? That, yes, I might be possibly thinking about something that's more important than you?"

"That's not how I meant it. I just wanted to know if you were fucking listening."

"Well, now I'm fucking listening." I cringe after saying it, but I'm tired. Every night ends the same way these days. With a stupid argument, maybe some meaningless hate sex, and falling asleep angry at each other.

"I already told you—Never mind. You were just on your own little planet. What *were* you thinking about?"

"Just something that happened with Dannie at a shoot."

He nods his head. "There we are. Anytime your head's in the clouds lately, it's always about Dannie. Did they grow a dick suddenly?"

Eric knows well enough by now that respecting their pronouns was absolutely non-negotiable. But he's starting to piss me off, more and more often. I wish that Dannie was here instead of him. They always know the right thing to say. I don't know what to make of these thoughts, but they exist. And I become lost in my dissociative pattern again.

"Okay, well, there you go again. Off on Planet Ashlin. I just asked you if you wanted to take a break. Now, I'm making that decision for you." He grabs his phone and some stuff from our bedroom, and without another word, walks out of the apartment, slamming the door. I nearly leap off the couch at the noise.

***

I wake up with a start. It's three in the morning, and my phone's about to die. But instead of charging it, I lie there, thinking about the dream that made me jolt awake from a deep sleep. I wipe my sweaty brow and pull the blanket closer to my neck, despite feeling hot. The dream hadn't made a lot of sense.

I was walking through a house. It was large and spacious with huge bay windows, just like the home I grew up in.

I walk by room after room, starting from the front door. I traveled down the hallway, my notes app open on my phone like I was looking at a property for the first time. The house had an office space, a huge open concept living room, four bedrooms… It was everything someone could want. Even a good price point.

But there wasn't any furniture. The more I explored, the emptier it felt. In all the doors I walked past there's a blank canvas of a room. Plain white walls, bland flooring, and no furniture or decor at all. My skin stung with cold, and I felt alone. I kept going because I could hear faint music playing. It was a soft, familiar indie song. The kind of thing I'd listen to while taking a bath and relaxing.

Where is it coming from? I kept walking, my steps filled with hesitation. Eyebrows lowered slightly in a furrow, I made my way toward the music.

Each step felt heavier by the second. I looked down and my ankles had weights around them, the kind some people used at the gym. And I noticed they were connected by chains.

Clunk. Clunk. Clunk. The chains rattled against the ground as I crept down a long hallway.

Finally, I entered the kitchen, the source of the music. As if by magic, the weights were gone. I stepped much into the room, feet feeling freer. It was bright, with open windows, and a warm breeze slowly surrounding me.

"Sorry, give me a sec."

I whipped around and recognized the voice.

There was one other person in the kitchen. They were wiping off the counters. "Jesus, sorry. It was a wreck in here."

Ding. The oven timer beeped.

The other person opened the oven, blue oven mitts on, and pulled out a tray of lemon poppyseed muffins. The sweet aroma filled the room, and I inhaled, smiling.

The other person said, "I never cook, but I figured, what the hell? I ought to try it every once in a while. I thought you'd like it."

I gulped. "I do."

We sit down to eat, and that's when I wake up, more confused than ever. My pulse races, and it takes a while to steady it. I sit up a bit, leaning against my pillow, then lying back down, indecisive. I take a few deep breaths and begin to grow more relaxed. I feel a heat between my legs that's pleasant, which confuses me even more. Something about the dream stirred something inside me that I haven't felt in a long time. Desire.

I find my hand trailing down toward the warmth like it had a mind of its own. The feeling only grows as I begin to explore. My fingers knead and caress and after a few minutes, my toes curl, and my body rocks with quick bursts of pleasure.

Afterwards, I wipe my hand on the sheets, reminding myself to wash them later. I lie there for several minutes, trapped in thought. This can't be about Dannie. It's just been too long since I've had good sex, and the dream threw me for a loop somehow. Eric luckily was sleeping on the couch.

It had been strange, though. Dannie baking me muffins? They've never baked a thing in their life, as far as I knew. At least not since we've known each other.

Sometimes, dreams try to tell you things that are buried in your subconscious. So I pulled out my phone, forgetting it was dying. Now it was dead.

After getting up and plugging it in by my desk, I sit at my computer and begin to google some of the things I remembered. An empty house. A cozy kitchen. Dannie pulling muffins out of the oven. There's a site I use on occasion when I have a weird dream.

I open it up and take out a notebook, writing *Empty house.* The website basically said: All houses represent yourself. An empty house means you feel empty inside and lonely. Cool. That's awesome. It wasn't untrue, but reading it in black and white like that left me feeling even worse about it. But, maybe the rest of the dream was better.

The kitchen part seems like a good thing. Positive changes... good omens... That's not so bad. Then I stop in my tracks, and I read the next sentence over and over again.

If you see yourself being with a woman in a kitchen, this means you will soon have some interesting experiences in your private life.

Dannie had been there, but they were non-binary. Genetically, they were female, but I've always been supportive of their gender identity. Dannie isn't a woman. They identified as neither a woman nor a man. Still. It's interesting. I definitely *could* use some changes in my personal life. Maybe they involved Dannie.

The thought makes my stomach flutter. First, there's the dream itself, now this. I keep reading. What the hell does baking muffins mean?

Positive changes... Freud said dreaming about food represents your libido. The muffins had been awesome. Jesus. The next bit says, *Baking in dreams can certainly become sensual: the act of eating is highly delicate and also intimate dinners frequently come before sexual intercourse.*

I exit out of the tab as quickly as I can. Do I have feelings for Dannie? Is that what this is all about? I've never been interested in women. Not even close. Then again, Dannie isn't a woman. But they look like one...

I'm so confused. I've always dated cisgender men. That felt comfortable to me.

I think back to some of my recent encounters with Dannie. The touches on the shoulder. The smirks. The sarcastic jokes. The help at work. Why did all that feel so comfortable, too?

We're close friends, sure. We support each other at work. Dannie was there to talk to when I was having a hard time. They've even been trying to make me feel included in their time with Rosa, and I know how precious that time is to Dannie.

The idea of them making muffins in the kitchen for me brings an unexpected smile to my face. The domesticity makes me feel so much less lonely. And they had tasted really good. Lemon poppyseed was my favorite. I can still taste them in my mouth.

Chapter 13

Charlie

September 2016

The scene is so damn grim, a slow walk through a dense forest leading to what I'm staring at now—the lifeless body of what was once a lovely young woman. Again. The decomp is already pretty advanced so we could only just make out her features. She has short dark hair that complements her narrow face and cheekbones I wish I had. She'd probably been beautiful, just like the others. Now, her eyes are almost completely opaque, and most of the teeth that once filled her mouth are missing.

"I have a daughter about her age," Agent Holloway tells me as we pace around the scene. "I'm about to be a grandfather for the first time. I see this shit, and I wonder when it'll be time."

"Time for what, Agent?"

"To take my pension and run." He allows himself a quiet chuckle, the volume appropriate despite the circumstances. "One day, instead of walking into these weekly horror shows, I'm going to walk into my daughter's house without needing to take a thirty minute long hot shower first, and snuggle that baby."

I smile. "Is it a boy or a girl?"

"She wants to be surprised." He rolls his eyes. "And she wants everything gender neutral." Even in our short professional relationship, I've grown to learn Agent Holloway is super old school. I try to change with the times, but that isn't always the case with men his age.

Changing the subject, he turns to the tech, and says, "See anything?"

The eager young tech, fresh out of school, says, "If I could guess manual strangulation was the COD, MOD homicide. There's the, uh…" He gestures toward his eyes.

I say, and give him a weak smile. "It's alright, kid. It takes time. You're doing good work. The coroner will be here in a bit to touch base and bring her back as soon as we're done walking the scene." After a pause, I say, "Petechial hemorrhaging."

The tech is once again fixated on taking pictures. He has to be thorough before more hands get on the body, and make sure he gets enough usable DNA samples. He pauses and says, "Ma'am?"

"That's what you were trying to say a minute ago. The thing with the eyes after a rough strangulation. Petechial hemorrhaging."

An awkward laugh escapes the tech's lips. "Right, sorry. I knew that. It's just… It's wild. It's like I know her."

"Yeah, it feels that way sometimes." I squat down, my knees cracking the way they hadn't even a year ago. Agent Holloway remains standing, watching my interaction with the kid. I stare at the bits of mud and river grass caked on her face. "You get this? Might be mud from the dumpsite."

"I got the soil samples before I started taking pictures. But I'm serious. I know she's kind of hard to make out right now, with the teeth and the eyes, but I swear I know her."

Holloway helps me up and says, "Oh yeah? Is she an ex of yours?"

He flushes. "No, she's… not my type, in that way." With a knowing nod from Holloway, the tech continues. "But she reminds me of this woman my partner works with. Sarah. She's really nice. Always bringing in coffee for people. Sometimes, we'd all go out for drinks. The vic reminds me of her. I'm just making an observation."

I pat him on the back. "That's great. That could be helpful. I'll let that one know." I jerk my head over to the right, where Agent Holloway now stands talking to the local district attorney. I walk over to Agent Holloway, and say, "The kid thinks he knows her. Might be some acquaintance from his boyfriend's work. Worth looking into, considering how little DNA this psycho left."

"Good. Do some digging and keep me in the loop. I'm gonna go back and set up shop in the meeting room. Another one to add to the board. We've got a serial on our hands. It's definitely not going to be the last time. At least we have *this* this time around." He holds up two evidence bags, collected by another tech. One contains a sock. The other contains a set of keys.

Him

September 2016

I can't help myself at this point. It's as strong a compulsion as washing your hands after using a disgusting truck stop bathroom. Or a night with a whore. Slathering your hands with soap and rinsing them off in scalding hot water. Feeling the burn of the water, the pain. Afterwards, you hate yourself for it, but you aren't able to stop.

That's what this feels like.

I wouldn't have to do any of this if I'd just been able to finish the job off last year. I was so disappointed in myself. At least that's what I think so I don't feel like a complete monster. I wasn't always this way. I had principles I lived by.

I'm standing across the street from a grocery store. The first woman I killed, with the music note keychain, had kids. I read that somewhere. I'm not a big fan of kids, but I don't like the idea of taking someone's mother away. Being without a mother is a fucking terrible feeling.

It's the rage about my failure that fills me like lava and makes me watch the others. If I watch them first and not act so carelessly, I can avoid any mistakes I made, whatever they might be.

I sit there, stewing, and then I see a woman walking out of the store. She's holding a single paper bag in her right arm and talking on her cell phone with the other hand. After a few minutes, she closes the cell phone and keeps walking east toward another strip mall. She looks both ways and crosses the street. I avert my gaze. I don't want her to know I'm watching, and watching with pleasure. She walks right past me, as I sit on the bench outside of a closed bookstore.

A warm breeze slides across my body and after a couple of minutes, I get up and start walking. Then a strange opportunity presents itself. One that could make the capture easy, but is riskier than I wanted. But I can feel my ears pounding, like I was standing in front of a booming speaker. I quicken my pace a little and approach her.

"Let me help you with that, ma'am." I pick up the groceries that the clumsy bitch dropped, as she thanks me profusely. She eyes me up and down and smiles.

"No problem at all." I'm not going to let her get away like *she* did. The rest has gotten so goddamn easy. It's a simple checklist I follow in my head.

Watch. Check.

Follow. Check.

Don't be a goddamn stereotype with the dark alleyways and shit. Check.

Use as few supplies as possible. Check.

Don't run your mouth. Check.

I'm getting pretty good at this.

***

Fuck. They found a sock. Months later, they finally stumbled across it. Must have gotten buried under some mud or leaves or some shit. I thought I'd been careful and covered my tracks better.

I close the newspaper, and throw it into a nearby garbage can at the park. The cops found something, and that's bad. It's only a sock. That's what I'm trying to tell myself. How much DNA could possibly be on a sock? I pop a pill into my mouth and swallow it dry. A little habit I picked up recently. At least it's not as bad as my other ones.

The cops still don't have a suspect, according to a reporter. So that's good news. But they've decided to keep the case open and they're going to search local nature preserves to see if there are more bodies. I should have mixed up the locations. They're going to be fixated on that now.

As much as the urge is growing impossible to fight, I have to try to fight it before I get caught. What could the cops find next? How else did I fuck up?

It's infuriating. That's how all of this started, my own self loathing. That's always been an ongoing issue of mine, being treated like a failure, especially by those close to me. Just rejection in general. These women walk around so carefree, life breezing past them as casually as the wind, and they never have to worry. They don't have to worry about what their families think. No one's treating them like they're nothing. They just *live*, and no matter how many you step on, there are a thousand more in their place.

It all started with a job interview, someone stepping into my office, not having any idea how life would turn out. It was just a temp job, and they could have not applied. We were redoing the website, and needed some help updating the About Us page. The fury settles again in my chest when I think about how rude they were, the kind of rudeness that time doesn't easily heal.

I can still feel that noise in my ears, and my fists clench in my lap. What the fuck was I thinking, starting all this in the first place? But you live and learn, and now I'm learning. I'm learning quickly that as my anger about my failure grows, the more I realize I need to do something about it. Even though this should never have started, there's no way to leave it unfinished.

I know I need to be more careful, but I don't feel strong enough to control myself. I want to live a normal life, free of emotional torment, but the thrill excites me. It makes me feel powerful and in control. I just need to figure out a way to move in closer. Make her trust me, and then yank it all away.

Well, I did one thing right. I moved the goddamn keychains into the vent last week. Before then I'd been keeping them in a box in the closet in my apartment like a moron, hoping no one came across them. The cops are sniffing around the Chalice case, and I need to make sure nothing can be tied back to me. And I'm pretty sure the vent can't.

But now they found a goddamn sock, buried under months of leaves and dirt and muck. Tangible evidence that could get me locked away forever. All I'd wanted was to make this feeling go away.

I fight back a scream. I'm desperate to let out years of sadness and sheer hatred. My life was ruined, my ego shattered into a million pieces. It was ruined as a child, but compounded one hundred fold the day the they told me I was scum, that there was no way in a million years anyone would fuck me if I stayed the way that I was. That hurt. It was like my mother always told me: I have to be exceptional or I won't ever get anywhere in life. Now, I'm failing yet again by my own careless actions.

I stare around the park at the mothers pushing their children in strollers, and people jogging, their lives so free from worry and pain. One day I can be like them, living a normal life just like I always wanted before these impulses started. I can live a clean life and be a good person. I just have to think this through, really consider my choices—*think before I act,* my mother's voice scolded me in my mind.

Another pill down the hatch. What the hell am I going to do?

Chapter 14

Dannie

April 2021

Ajingling fills my ears, like a macabre set of Christmas bells, which makes my skin crawl. I envision faceless monsters standing outside my door, seen through the security eye hole, singing *Santa Claus Is Coming To Town*. My eyes blink open, and my vision is blurry. When it clears, someone's dangling the set of keychains in my face. A man, unrecognizable from blurriness, is lying on top of me, propped up on his elbows. I can feel his waist pressed against mine, and I wiggle under his weight.

He dangles them so close to my eyes that they become out of focus again. I squint to see and try to continue making out the face. It was oval-shaped, with brown hair. What color eyes does he have? What about his build? His clothes? Nothing else stands out.

I try squinting again and after a few seconds, I can almost make his eyes out. They were round, and... Damn it. All of it's gone blank. All I can see is a vague outline of where a face should be, like the carolers wishing me a merry little Christmas.

I'm so close. I can almost see his face. It's just been a momentary glimpse, not too quick to notice any distinct features. Now, it's just the noise I can make out. *Jingle. Jingle. Jingle.* And the smell. He smelled like something I couldn't place. Like a cheap cologne. My nose scrunches up in disgust, and it's difficult not to gag. I feel a soft plush object rub against my face. I squint and it's something purple hanging from the keychains. It's one of them. The lucky rabbit's foot.

"Get off me, asshole!" Dream Me pushes and shoves against his weight as hard as I can. After several minutes, my muscles ache with exhaustion.

"If only it were that simple. I'm not making the same mistake again." His voice is bubbling poison, and I shrink back more with every word. I recognize his voice. I've known him for years. My heart races, and he pours vodka down my throat from my own flask. It's so heavy, I nearly drown.

Then the scene changes. I must have fought him off. Now, Dream Me is in bed, but a different one. The silky, smooth sheets rub against my skin. I try to sit up, but I'm met with a "Ssshhhhh. It's okay." The voice is as soft as the sheets and is inches away from my ear.

The other person's breath is warm, whispering comforting platitudes, and I feel their arms wrap around me. My body goes limp with relaxation, my heart rate slowing, and my breathing slower and slower as I gain realization. Of course. It's Ashlin lying next to me, green eyes looking into mine, a smile playing on her lips. We're facing each other and she has one arm under my neck and the other lying gently across my waist.

Her hand grazes my arm, and the last thing I hear before I wake up is, "You're going to die, bitch."

My eyes shoot open and my mouth hangs down like it's on a broken hinge. I can't fucking breathe. It takes several minutes before my heart rate calms down and I can see more than just a narrow tunnel in front of me, the blurriness gradually receding.

I take a deep breath and think about the dream. The same man again. I choke back bile thinking about it now, especially. Not choking me this time, but taunting me with the keychains we found. Shit. The purple rabbit's foot. It all comes crashing back on me. The gift from Rosa when I moved to Chicago. She'd thought I needed some luck in a new city. The fucking irony. I lost it pretty quickly after, and Rosa told me, "I guess I'll be your lucky charm then."

I didn't lose it. He must have taken it at some point. How else would he have it? Or is that just the dream messing with me? I'm so confused.

The voice is his, I know it, and I shiver under the bedsheets. Why would I dream about him doing something like that? Assuming the dreams are based in fact, and Christ, I hope not. I make a vow to myself to never tell her, unless it comes up by itself. If I find out it's true, and I'm willing to press charges, I'll have to break the news as gently as possible. I don't like lying, but I need to be one hundred percent sure first.

I hate these dreams but oddly, I yearn for more, for a better understanding of what happened to me. Something must have happened to me.

I reach for my flask and take a hearty gulp, despite the dream vodka being unpleasant. I need something to numb the chaos in my mind, and I chase it with a pill from my little bag. I'm going to need more. I know I definitely have a problem but I'm not ready to let it go. I've convinced myself it's the only thing keeping me from daily panic and irritability.

Then there's the part with Ashlin. Of course, I recognize *her* voice. I shudder, remembering the way Ashlin's hand felt against my arm, her breath making my stomach flutter. She'd been so close to my ear that I'd felt her lips graze my skin, and I tremble thinking about it. My heart races again and I mutter obscenities. I am so fucked up.

***

The same dream, or an extremely similar variation, continues the next few nights. The only difference is that every night the jingles get louder and the man's face becomes slightly clearer. The second night his features have outlines, and the next night I can see his eyes staring down at me. In the same dreams, Ashlin's touch grows fonder and more insistent. Her caresses are firmer, and her legs graze against mine like we'd done this a million times. When I think back to it, my eyes close, trying to commit it to memory as well as I can since it's probably never going to actually happen.

Ugh, the goddamn keychains. They haunt me. They could be innocent, or sinister, or somewhere in between. More likely, they're worth forgetting altogether, but it didn't stop my obsessive brain from spiraling.

And if I think too hard about the steamy Ashlin parts of the dreams, I might be compelled to act on these feelings that are growing by the day, and that would be an awful idea. Like a romance novel gone horribly wrong. The protagonist left heartbroken, head in their palm, tears streaming down their face.

This shit's going to chew me up like a moth on an old sweater. It comes down to what part is more important to me right now—the keychains, or how I feel about Ashlin. The choice should feel more obvious than it does. Shouldn't it?

***

The next night, like clockwork, I wake up and can't breathe. I try to reach for my flask but I'm stuck in place. My arms are glued to my sides, and I can barely sit up. Sobs escape my lips in loud bursts, tears streaming down my face. I manage to grab the pillow next to me and scream into it at the top of my lungs. The more I think about it, this is the kind of thing that happened to Marco when he got back, and my brain's too foggy to remember what to do.

What the fuck what the fuck what the fuck…

I can't stop crying and my body is trembling uncontrollably. I attempt to take a few deep breaths and barely manage to fill my lungs. Tears splash down onto my hand, and I yank my phone off the nightstand. Fingers shaking, I send out a text to my emergency contact and drop the phone on the ground.

The text is short, all I can manage to type between gasps:

Help.

It's that goddamn dream. I can't stop thinking about it. Him leaning over me, his hair damp with sweat, beads of it dripping onto my forehead. His eyes are filled with lust and hatred, and they seem to smile at me when I yell.

I scream into the pillow again, and my body can't stop shaking. Tears are flowing so hard that the pillow's drenched. My chest rises and falls in rapid bursts, tightness gripping it like a fist. Like his fist as he slams his hand on the bedside table in the dream.

In the dream, I'd jolted upright, gasping for air. I could see him, slamming his fist down twice and yelling, "What the fuck is your problem?"

My pants kept around my ankles, fighting hard as he climbs on top of me again. Him pinning me down is now a part of the dream every night.

It's rushing back to me, in short bursts of horror, and I fall off the bed, my head hitting the floor. I remember it all—the pain, the fear, the hopes that I could just die instead. Why did he do this to me, and when? Was it before or after?

Stars cloud my vision, and the trembling becomes worse. My body pulses with sadness. I try to stay conscious, but things are slipping away fast. I must have hit my head harder than I thought. The last thing I think before I pass out is, Why?

***

Who knows how long later, I come to and hear a set of keys frantically working in my doorknob. My heart skips a beat and I groan, trying to get the energy to call out. My body is still lying helpless on the floor, just as I see feet running into my bedroom.

I look up and see a blurry face leaning over me, crying. A minute later, they rest my head in their lap and put an ice pack on my head. Normally I try to reserve that treatment for the worst hangovers. I feel the person's tears land on my forehead, and I sit up with a jolt.

"Don't touch me! Don't fucking touch me!" My gasping breaths resume, and the impulse to scream is nearly impossible. "Don't touch me."

My vision clears and I see Rosa. Rosa's face sags, her eyes dark and knowing. This isn't the first time I'd lashed out at Rosa, but it had never been this bad. And never the result of a dream.

Rosa keeps holding the ice pack, and her lips quiver as she chokes back more tears. She looks at me, her eyes searching for an explanation.

I gag and say, "Just—just gimme…" I run into my bathroom and dry heave into the toilet, gripping the icy porcelain with shaky arms. My stomach too empty for vomit, the nausea comes in painful waves. I resume my crying spell, and put my head between my knees. Why am I like this? I hate it so much, and it makes me hate myself. There are so many days I wish I could disappear. It makes me wonder why people like Rosa and Ashlin even bother. I hit myself on the head with my palm once, twice, three times.

Rosa grabs my hand, and begins rubbing my back. Her voice is soft. "Deep breaths. Deep breaths. In and out. In and out."

Without lifting my head, I take a deep breath and blow it out. Or, at least, I try. I pick up my head. I feel totally checked out, like I've just been through hell and am too numb to process it.

Rosa, trying to be as soothing as possible, says, "This has happened before, Dan. Maybe not to this extreme. But the anger and the tears, dozens of times over the past several years. Just like with Marco. And I don't know how to save either of you. He tried therapy, remember, and it went out the window the second he met that asshole, Tony."

She looks at me and continues, "I love you, and have been *trying* to get your ass to talk to a therapist for years. Maybe it would work for you. It's the flask, and the pills, the sobbing, the flying off the handle." Rosa's chest rises and falls with every word, and she points a finger at me. A second later, she lowers it, and buries her own head in her knees and cries. "I can't take it anymore."

My breathing is just about back to normal, and I wipe away the last of my tears. "I try to hide it well. I swear. It's just easier to let my guard down in front of you since we've known each other for so long. I'm scared it's going to affect my job, and things with Ashlin. Things are so fucking complicated. The vodka and the pills help but—" I shrug. "—it's getting worse, and I don't know how to make it stop. I can't take it anymore, either."

Rosa manages to become steady and calm. "You could go to one of Marco's meetings with him. Lord knows he needs a good influence. And you could talk to him about your experience coming out. He's really been struggling with his identity, too. Having to live in secret. You need help, love. Real help. As in not a bottle of disgusting, shitty ass bottom-shelf liquor."

I feign a smile. "Well, I'm not a high roller like you." I close my eyes. "I had a dream. There was a man there. Brown hair. I don't know. Average height, weight, whatever. His eyes were… horrifying." I gulp. "He was doing things to me. I don't know what exactly, but my pants were down…"

I start to cry again, and lean my head on Rosa's shoulder. I look up, my head still resting there, and Rosa's eyes are blinking over and over as if the wheels are turning in her head. I'm such a goddamn failure. I can't shake these feelings. The anger. Can't stop with the flask. What the hell is wrong with me?

I must have said the last part out loud, because Rosa says, "There's nothing wrong with you. You're a great person. I'm going to sit on the bed and let Ashlin know what's going on, and tell her you'll be okay."

I nod and she helps me to my feet. She says, "Alright, take a minute while I text her. Come over here and sit next to me. We're gonna get this figured out, love."

Rosa tucks me in under the covers and fluffs the pillows. After Rosa messages Ashlin, I lean back and say, "Something happened to me. I don't know what. I don't know when. But it was at that goddamn house." I turned to face her. "The one with the keychains."

In full mom mode, Rosa says, "First and foremost, we're finally going to get you a therapist, dumbass." I flinch and Rosa waves her hands in front of her. "Sorry, that was harsh. I'm not mad. Obviously. I'm just... scared. You fucking scared me bad. And now this dream you're having? What's up with that? I wouldn't know, I'm not a therapist. So, just get one already. Okay?"

"I don't know. Can you have something happen to you and totally forget?" I ask her, my voice quiet. I'm afraid that if I speak louder he'll hear me, somehow, no matter how far away he is.

Rosa takes out her phone again and begins typing furiously. She raises a finger and says, "I found something that talks about trauma. It can affect your memory. Some people I guess forget who they are entirely, but that's super rare." She scans the text. "Usually the memory loss doesn't last long, but it can depend on the person or the incident. It's more likely if you've had other trauma or abuse in the past."

I bite my lip, and nod. "Well, as you know, my saint of a mother said, 'I don't know any Dannie.'"

My voice shakes. I'm so sick of crying. I tell Rosa the story as if it was the first time, and she listens patiently. "After decades of being my mother, she looked right at me, and she didn't know who I was. Or what. And what's worse, she didn't care." I sniffle, and say, "She didn't make any attempt to get to know me. To try to love me the way that I am."

I gulp and put my head on Rosa's shoulder again. "I know you. So does Ashlin. And what's more, we love you for you. Busted ass fashion and all."

I smirk. "I like wearing black. It's better than your fucking floral nightmares."

We laugh. Then I sigh. I don't know what I'd do if not for the two of them. Rosa's phone pings multiple times in rapid succession. "What did Ashlin say?"

"Let me try to summarize. It's the equivalent of a frat boy group text, but with only her. What's wrong? Is Dannie okay? Oh my God, what if something's wrong? Should I call 911? Are they hurt?" With a sarcastic laugh, Rosa says, "Basically, she's *exasperated with worry*, as she puts it. You might want to text her before she calls a SWAT team."

I smile and grab my phone from Rosa's outstretched hand. She knows my phone code, and already has my text thread with Ashlin pulled up. I tell her things are okay, and no, she doesn't need to come over, and I'll live. What I really mean is, I don't know if I can process my feelings when she's around. They just get more complicated.

I think about him- the man from the dream. Were there others? Did he do it because he hates me, or because he hates himself? More importantly, was any of this even real? I close my eyes as Rosa strokes my hair.

***

"Ro told me to stop answering your texts," he says, looking around as if Rosa's lurking behind the corner.

I lock the door behind him. "I know. She told me to stop texting you. But I need help. Like you did after Afghanistan. And until I can get more money together to get it on a regular basis, the pills and vodka are the only things that actually help." If anyone would understand it, Marco would. Spending money on drugs then complaining you can't afford therapy, when deep inside you're just too afraid. We aren't super close, but he's dealt with the same kinds of feelings.

"It's bad enough, the way things are going with Tony. We're still hiding from the family, and we've been fighting more. I don't want any drama. I came by to check on you because you seem like you're in a bad way again. I'm trying to get clean. You know that, right?" I nod, and

Marco continues. "I'm trying to work on things with Tony. I just got a new job. Maybe you can help me figure out a way to be more open with my family? I don't know."

"Of course, Marco. I'd be happy to help. I know how hard it is when your family's not ready to listen."

He dodges my response and says, "The pills are good money, but I need to cut this shit out."

"So do I," I say. "Just one more time. Please?"

He sighs and hands me a bag. "This is my last bag. The last time. Got it? And maybe it's better if you don't text me. The less time I spend with you, the less chance I have of running into Eric. I swore I'd never speak to him again, and I can't break that promise to myself. I've already broken so many fucking others."

Him

There she is. I pop a pill into my mouth, my last one. I sigh and keep watching. She's standing outside of the agency, talking to Dannie and the receptionist. They're laughing, and I wish I knew what the joke was.

She's special. Special enough to catch Dannie's eye at least. I know how close they are. Every time I watch her, I wonder how she has it so easy. After all I've been through, all the shit I saw over there, no one should be able to go through life like that. All smiles, casual arm touches, and hair flips.

I've known her for a while now and know that most of it's crap. She's one of those people who puts on a pretty face, luring flies with honey, and all that. Beneath the surface, however, lies a person who wants to be loved but doesn't know how to go about doing that.

The group breaks up, and I lower my head. I'm across the street but don't want to be seen by Ashlin or Dannie. I watch them walk away in my periphery and wonder how I can finally end this.

Chapter 15

Rosa

May 2021

We walk toward a familiar broken neon sign. As we do, a prickle runs down my neck. The kind I get when Mama catches me on my phone in church. I turn around and briefly lock eyes with someone. Oh it's him. Fantastic. Cue the drama. I glare at him, and we walk inside after an elbow nudge from Ashlin. Apparently, Ashlin's been talking.

"Come back to Earth, Rosa. We said we'd meet at eleven, so let's go in. We all know how much you like punctuality. I was late for drinks one time."

Dannie smiles. "It's a cardinal sin. Can't fault her for her innate and unhealthy obsessions."

I roll my eyes as we walk in. I know it's true and start to laugh, but I'm too damn annoyed that he's here to make much of an effort. We've been trying to avoid him as much as possible.

Luckily, Ashlin takes the bait, like she usually does. She laughs and looks at Dannie, her eyes warm and crinkling at the corners. "I'm glad you're smiling."

Dannie returns the look and says, "I am, too."

The dreams have been haunting all of us, the thought of one of us being assaulted by someone. Dannie's been acting all secretive, like they know more about the dreams than they're letting on. I wonder—Was Dannie hurt by someone? Who? When? Why? I'm desperate for them to heal. I want them to seek help.

Only I know about the other parts of the dreams. Dannie finally caved after a few too many drinks. I've been trying to stop enabling their drinking problem, and it makes me feel awful, but I know they need to open up more, and that's one way to get them to do it. I feel guilty prick at me for allowing them to indulge. But I wanted to know if there was anything I could do. Any way I could help. I wanted them to talk to me. They did—Dannie's been fantasizing about Ashlin. A hand sliding up an arm. The gentle touches of lovers, not friends.

I wish that was the entirety of the dreams, not the sick, terrifying shit that went along with it. It probably feels good to at least have the pleasant parts of the dream to cling to between the horrors surrounding the happiness. Or maybe that part just makes Dannie feel worse.

We walk to our regular booth, the one we always sit at once a week on my lunch break. As we get closer, I wave to the server, Lila, a really sweet younger woman that usually has our table.

"Been on any good dates recently?" she asks me, a smile lighting up her face.

"No. Not even a goddamn nibble. God, what I'd give for a nibble…" I let the sentence drift away as Lila walks away, and my eyes look Dannie and Ashlin's way. They have their heads together, and they're laughing. "Hey, you two. You. *Two.*" My eyes then flash a message at Dannie that Dannie could damn well read. "Anyway, I was just telling Lila that the dating game is a bust lately," I say, as if I could make the conversation turn to a lighter topic.

Lila waves from a couple tables away, notepad out, heading into the throngs of busy people hiding from their bosses while they eat a quick lunch.

We all sit down, Dannie and Ashlin on one side, Ashlin toward the inside of the booth. I sit on the other side. Of course I do. Ashlin makes a show of setting her purse down and looking for the perfect place to store her cellphone. I roll my eyes. "It's alright, girlfriend. I don't mind being a third wheel. How are things with Prince Eric? I'm in the dry spell of the century."

Ashlin lets a quiet laugh escape her lips. Dannie shoots daggers at me, and Ashlin shrugs. "Uh, nothing new. Just staying busy at work. Ships passing in the night and all that," she says, digging back into her purse.

I raise my eyebrows. "Well, you've been together a while now."

Ashlin clears her throat and says, "Yeah... Okay, anywho, I did some googling about your dreams to see if I could help us to understand them better. I didn't really find much. I searched for missing people, and keychains. Any combination of keywords I could think of." She looks at Dannie, and tucks a strand of hair behind her ear. "You mentioned looking it up, right?"

The look was that of two people who've spent years together, talking about their days at work and snuggling up on the couch. Except they both seem surprised by it. "Yeah, I looked it up, too. Not much in my results either. I did find something that said, 'Four women missing- no phones, wallets, or keys left behind.'" I recall the article title as a familiar chill runs over me before I continue, "They found a woman named Melissa with her keys missing."

I take a sip of the water the busser put in front of me and add my two cents. "Maybe that has something to do with it then?" I look at Dannie to gauge her reaction.

"A lot of people go missing each year, and even more people commit crimes. How would we ever have a way of narrowing something down to four keychains? I don't know why I thought this was so sinister. Maybe I watch too much TV. Everything is a hidden clue." Dannie waggles her fingers like a magician trying to fool an audience.

Lila comes back to the table, and we order lunch and a cocktail each.

I say, "It's fucking weird, though. Wonder why the guy even left them there. It is a guy who owns the house, right?"

"Yeah, it's a guy," Ashlin says. "If he was even the one who left them. We hardly know anything about him. He calls periodically to check in, and we know he wants it relisted, but he says he doesn't live in the area anymore, so—"

Dannie's eyes shoot up from their lap and say, "It was him. In the dream. The one from all the dreams. They take place in his house." A dark expression flickers across Dannie's face, and they look like they're going to puke. I make a mental note to find out what the hell is going on.

Ashlin takes a drink and holds her hands up, "Alright, this is starting to scare me. Do you still have the keychains?" Dannie nods. "Should we, I don't know, do something with them? Like turn them in to the cops? Could there be some trace DNA or something on them?"

Trying to put aside Dannie's weirder than normal behavior—which we're for sure going to talk about later—I suppress a grin and say, "You never know. It happens on *Dateline*."

Dannie snaps, "Oh come on. It is *odd*, like I said. But let's not go from zero to Keith Morrison okay? I'll just hang on to them. Maybe they're important, or maybe I'm just making a big deal out of nightmares and keychains."

"Okay, fine. Ashlin, cutie pie, don't get Dannie into trouble at work over this. And I know, I know. Vice versa. Let's pump the brakes for now. That being said, I'm worried about you, love. The dreams, the weird vibes, the PTSD attacks."

Dannie sighs and rolls their eyes. "PTSD attacks," they mumble.

The food comes and we dig in, but not with much excitement or hunger.

"I'm serious. You know that Marco was in Afghanistan. He had awful dreams, snapped at people for no reason, tried to cope by popping pills." I say the last few words pointedly as if each one was a separate sentence.

"He gets anxious all the time. Therapy and meds worked for a while, but he almost killed himself a few years ago. He tried again a couple months later. I know you remember that. So, please, promise me you'll be careful. I have a bad feeling myself now, about these dreams, and those keys."

Dannie makes a scout's promise hand gesture, but their eyes meet mine knowingly. They know how broken up I am about Marco. And how scared I was after the nightmare.

"Make sure Find My Phone is turned on. Always. And going forward, text me every day and let me know what's going on with you."

"I always text you and tell you what's going on," Dannie says. Bullshit.

"It's a good idea," Ashlin says, which I very much appreciate. "I've been worried, too. Text us and fill us in on how things are going. Not just what you had for breakfast or how empty your flask is." She swats Dannie in the arm.

"Fine. I promise to text you both. With flaskless info."

I lift up the remainder of my gigantic BLT and we finish eating. When we're done, we talk a little more. Ashlin's looking at Dannie differently today. There's some kind of sparkle in her eyes. I don't know what that's all about. I say, "Alright, I'm gonna bypass the elephant in the room and dip out. This week's on me." I wave Lila over, who brings us the check.

The arm swat, the extra smiles. I can read Dannie's mind, like usual. How long would it be before it was impossible for one of us to stay silent about one of the few things going on in our friend group?

Ashlin's phone pings. She reads a text message and gasps as she glances to the right. I follow her gaze when her jaw drops to the floor.

There was Prince Eric, sitting at a table across the restaurant. We'd been so caught up in conversation, I hadn't noticed him there. He waves at us and turns back to his companion, the pretty red-headed coworker that Ashlin's vented about more than once. I'm assuming that's Stella. What was he doing with her?

"I hope to Christ that's a work lunch," I say, my fist tightening.

Ashlin shakes her head, a tear running down her cheek. "We've been fighting a lot. And he just texted me. *If you can go on dates, so can I*, it says."

"Prince Eric said *what* now?"

Dannie's eyes narrow. "Dates? What the fuck is he talking about?"

Another tear and Ashlin says, "He's mad that I talk about you so much. He thinks, you know, there's something going on. Even though he knows—" Her cheeks and neck flush.

Dannie puts her hand on Ashlin's. "I know. We're just friends. It's okay."

"Alright, screw it." I stand up, sick of all the bullshit in my life. It's way too much for one person to deal with and I can solve this problem pretty damn fast. Legs on fire, I storm over to Eric's table. Him and his overly gelled hair. His bad cologne you could smell from Ohio. His smug smile as I approach.

"Hi, Rosa. What's new?"

I lower my voice and set my hands on the table. "What's new with you, Eric?" I say it through gritted teeth, like his name is a swear word. I push down harder and look at his table mate. "Stella, was it?"

"Have we met?" Stella looks at me nervously.

"Didn't need to, don't want to. Look Eric, I know you and Marco have a history. Oorah and all that." I look back at Stella. "He and my cousin were Marine buddies, and Eric's dating one of my friends in case you forgot." Now back to Eric. "Quit being a dick." I turn on my heels and start walking away.

Before I know what's happening, he's behind me, his breath hot on my neck. "You don't know anything about what happened over there. And you need to mind your own business. This is between me, Ashlin, and Dannie."

I feel a lump forming in my throat as he puts his hand on the back of my head, running it down the nape of my neck, lingering at its base. "Now go away. You don't want to make things worse."

Chapter 16

Ashlin

May 2021

I'm fuming, sitting behind my desk mindlessly responding to emails. My face feels hot, and I'm making poor attempts to not clench my jaw too hard. I hit send immediately after realizing I'd mixed up *their* and *there* a couple of times. Oh, screw it. I lean back in my chair, and wish I had a fan in here.

He'd looked so smug, sipping a beer with Stella, laughing so carelessly at one of her jokes. It was all made worse by the glances over at me as we rushed to pay the bill and leave, the looks that said *I win*. This is how I've seen it ending up for a long time and here it is. Him winning, and me being left behind like bones in the woods, picked at by vultures.

I feel really grateful for Rosa. She didn't need to confront him. That was beyond nice of her. After all, it was a problem between me and Eric. I'm glad that Rosa's letting me into the inner circle of her and Dannie's friendship a bit more, and I like it there.

People could learn a thing or two from Rosa. Rosa's kind and generous, but she's also tough and tells it like it is, and unabashedly loyal to those she loves. I'm glad to know her. What my mind would remember forever, however, wasn't that unpredictable display of loyalty. It was Dannie sitting next to me, holding my hand, telling me things would be okay.

Between that and the dream I had, my mind is a ball of yarn, unfurling more by the day. I shove the keyboard to the side and lay my head in my arms. Not crying, just mad and tired. I'm tired of feeling like I don't have what I want or deserve.

What's most maddening is that I'm coming to a deeper realization of what that is and I don't know how to set the yarn ball right again.

All of a sudden, I hear a noise in the lobby that makes me pick my head up. Kim's arguing with someone. I get out of my chair, and my feet take quiet steps closer to the door. With every step, the voices get louder and I press my ear to the wall.

"I'm sorry, Cheri's not here. She's at a closing and has another one after that. She might not be in at all the rest of the day."

"You can't call her? Leave a message. Isn't that your job?"

My hand touches on the doorknob, but I pull it back like I would from a sizzling frying pan. Instead, I keep listening.

"My job," Kim says, with a surprising level of attitude, "is to tell people like you to get the hell out. I'm not going to let you just stomp in here in your suit and talk to me like that. And by the way, the sleeves look a bit long."

I can feel Eric's rage building even through the door. "Well, is *she* here then?"

"She's out with a client right now."

"Bullshit. I could hear her walking around in her office just now."

I wince, and debate whether or not I should open the door. I want to defend Kim's honor, the way Rosa had defended mine, and of course I'm furious. But here I am cowering, considering hiding under my desk. Of course I am.

When did things get like this? My hiding from him in my office and him screaming at my colleagues. What's the final straw? If it isn't this, then I really don't want to know what is.

Of course, it's all about Dannie. My friendship with them is a source of anger for Eric that I can't lessen no matter how hard I try, and I don't want to. Dannie matters to me. Dannie, who held my hand while Eric humiliated me at the restaurant, who always answers my texts when Eric and I are fighting. I open the door and step out.

"What the hell, Eric? What's going on?"

"What's going on is your friend embarrassed me in front of Stella." His chest heaves and the vein in his forehead pulses.

I shake my head. This is it. I've had enough. He is *never* going to make me happy. He hasn't in a while, and after this, there's no going back and fixing things. "Do you hear how idiotic that sounds? She embarrassed you while you were out to lunch with the coworker we both know you're attracted to. Conveniently right after we have a major fight. Alright."

I throw my hands up. I can do one of two things. The thing I've always done, which was to try to placate and patch things up. That's what my mom would tell me to do. Or I could be brave, like Rosa, or Kim. Like Dannie who'd held my hand right in plain sight of my boyfriend. The choice was finally clear. "We're done. Get the fuck out, Eric. And get your shit out of my apartment."

Kim slowly backs up behind her desk and picks up the phone. Eric shoots her a look that could have killed her had the energy come from his fists. Kim puts it down on the receiver, and sits down, her eyes pleading with me, apologizing.

"I don't see you leaving," I say.

Eric lunges at me, pressing me up against the wall. "Where is this coming from? This attitude, this... Whatever this is. Is it something Dannie taught you the last time you fucked?"

I try to shove back against him, but he's too strong. "You think we had sex? That's what this is all about?" Suddenly, I'm more furious than I ever thought possible. Three years of my life wasted trying to make this narcissist happy. I'm different now, changed forever by a single encounter at a diner and by a thousand smaller moments with Dannie before that.

He lowers his voice, his face an inch or two from me. "She—they were holding your hand. Don't think I didn't see it."

I thrash under his grasp, while Kim picks up the phone again. "Put it down, Kim. It's okay. I can handle him. Yeah, they were holding my hand. And what if we *did* have sex? I'm sure it would be better than any sex I've had in a really long time."

He leans in so close that his nose is touching mine, his breath thick with alcohol.

"You can't call dibs on me anymore, you spoiled little prince." I laugh. "That's what Rosa calls you. Prince Eric. I'm not yours. And I never will be again. I'm theirs."

My face burns as his hand claps against my cheek. An angry cry escapes my lips as his hand lingers on my neck before dropping. Eric gives me one last look before walking out. He smooths the sleeves of his suit, and says, "You think I don't know that?"

Chapter 17

Charlie

May 2021

My manicured nails tap against my desk, thinking about Agent Peterson's latest email. The Feds are reopening the riverbed strangulation series from several years ago, after thousands of calls from desperate families about other missing women. No leads have ever come up. No common acquaintances. No usable DNA. Nothing.

Peterson's doing me a favor and flying out from DC to help me sort through this mess. The media just got wind that the case is reopening. The headlines are all over the place.

Stay safe- killer on the loose.

Who is The Riverbed Slayer?

Are these love affairs gone wrong?

I want to bang my head against the wall. The Riverbed Slayer. Jesus Christ. Why do people always name them? Doesn't the media know these psychos get off on that? I refuse to call him by a stupid nickname. To me, he's just a man, and one I intend to catch as quickly as possible.

My mind is running in circles as I wait for Peterson's telltale triple rap on the door. So far, we have Melissa Henrike. The second was Heather Cobi. Same MO. Manual strangulation, seeing as there were no signs of ligature marks. The third was Stephanie Aspen, followed by Sarah Chalice. At the Chalice scene, we'd found a sock, but the DNA was minimal and hadn't made a hit in the system. Then there'd been a few others since that they'd been unable to identify.

Right now, I feel like I've failed them. I always beat myself up about unsolved cases. These poor women, with no connection to each other. They appear to be random victims, taken from their families by a psychopath, just kicked into the river like trash. I have to fight to stop myself from crying.

I jump as someone knocks on my door. Three raps. Classic Chris. I subconsciously smoothe my hair and get up to let him in.

"Lieutenant," he says, strolling in and planting himself in a chair. He touches the gold placard on the front of my desk. "Still takes some getting used to."

"You're not kidding." I sit in the chair next to him, rather than the power move of sitting behind my desk. Our knees touch, and I should pull them away, but I can't resist the urge to let them linger.

"Thanks for getting back to me so quickly. The families are really sweating."

Chris rolls his eyes. "The Riverbed Slayer. Fuck me. These idiots never learn. Any updates? A hit on the sock?"

I sigh and say, "Zilch. So just a useless sock and a few sets of keys. Last body was found a few years ago, mid 2018."

"What are the families saying?"

"They want to know who killed their loved ones. And they're scared when we tell them this person might have hurt someone else. They did say something helpful, though." After a beat, I say, "We showed the keys we found to the Henrikes for identification purposes. Her husband said something curious." I wait to see if this attempt to bait Chris will work. It's one of my favorite pastimes.

Irritated, Chris says, "Out with it. What did he say?"

"Melissa's husband said they were her keys for sure—matched up with his house key and whatnot—but there was something missing. He said she always had a keychain on there, a music note. She loved that thing. Got it at work at the local music shop, and her job meant the world to her. She taught kids and stuff. He asked why all the keys were there, albeit a little rusty, but the music note was gone."

I let myself exhale. This was our latest development, and I hoped to hell it would lead to something. There's still no mention of keychains in the database in relation to missing women. No real mention of them at all. Maybe it did fall off in the water, knocked loose by the current and the rocks that lined the river bed. Pessimism comes naturally when cold cases are involved. I pick up my coffee and take a long chug, hands shaking. I need to kick my caffeine habit one of these days. But having Chris here feels exhausting. I'm glad for his help, but the lingering feelings my body keeps reminding me of aren't professional by any means. We haven't slept together in months, but I miss him and know I shouldn't.

"Fuck me," he says, scrolling through some notes on his phone. "Heather's girlfriend said the same thing when we did a follow up. Her keys washed up and they were missing a lucky pair of dice. I completely forgot."

I choke on my coffee and it takes a minute to get control of myself.

"You okay, Lieutenant?"

"Yeah. Yeah." I bring my hand to my throat and say, "I'm fine, just shocked. So Heather... she was missing a keychain, too?"

"Right. I'm not a huge believer in coincidences, but I don't want to rule anything out either. Alright, time to go add this to the board."

We head toward the meeting room that currently holds all the case files for the missing women. As I walk, I hear a sound at the front desk. I turn and see it's an angry woman with short dark hair demanding to speak to a supervising officer. She's with a blonde woman about the same age, and another with long dark hair. I walk over to see what the trouble is.

"What's going on, ladies?" I say. "This is homicide. Are you here to report a murder?"

The one with the short dark hair says, "It's they/them. For me. Anyway, we tried to go to another department but they were swamped. Their words, not mine."

My eyes crinkle and I feel like an asshole, but I didn't know. "I'm sorry about the 'ladies' thing then. What's your name?"

"Dannie, and this is Ashlin and Rosa." The blonde woman's eyes are red and she has a red mark on her face that appears to be the result of a hard slap.

I frown and look at Ashlin. "You okay, sweetie? Like I said, this is homicide but maybe I can help. I'm the lieutenant here. My name is Charlie. Do you want to come into my office and talk?"

We sit and Ashlin recounts the incident at the office. Dannie's angry and Rosa's face is like stone, her eyes blank with exhaustion. Ashlin begins crying, telling me about the assault by her now ex-boyfriend. Dannie lashes out at the mentions of him with phrases like, *How could he? What the hell? I'm gonna kick his ass.* They intersperse vengeful comments during the whole conversation, and also looks of fear.

As Ashlin talks, I take notes on a notepad. "I'm going to file a report and make sure it gets into the right hands. Is there anything else you want me to add?" I ask, my eyes still on my notepad.

Ashlin gulps and says, "Uh, right before he left, he put his hand on my throat. I thought he was going to choke me."

I look up. He almost choked her? The age fits our profile. Of all the gin joints, as they say. Could this be another coincidence? Like the keychains? No way could I get this lucky after so long, unless this *was* my lucky day, and I'd found a potential lead to look into. I need to keep a tab open on this one. Ashlin continues wiping the tears from her eyes. Dannie looks like she wants to say something but is holding back. I make a note to circle back to that as soon as I can. "It's gonna be okay, Ashlin. I'm gonna have a detective talk some more with you while I look into this some more. Chris?" I call out, my tone frantic and loud. "My office, now. And close the door."

Chapter 18

Dannie

May 2021

I wiggle in the soft suede chair and my entire body tenses up like there's a huge spider sitting next to me. I keep my eyes fixed there, like any moment it's going to leap up and start gnawing on my face. The clock says 8:07 and I'd give anything to have my flask here. But I made myself a promise, and I need to actually keep it for once. No more flask. Well, less flask.

I can't stand the thought of disappointing Rosa, and especially Ashlin. I think about Ashlin constantly, and I'm terrified that I'm falling in love. Or worse, I already am in love and am just going to end up getting hurt. But how can I keep being her close friend without wanting to get closer?

I realize I've been lost in thought and I take a long deep breath. I know what she asked me. Just didn't want to answer it at the time. I hate shrinks. But, I finally answer the therapist's question. "For as long as I can remember. At least the last several years. I think I've always had anxiety, but not this bad until I moved here."

Her lips curl up into a kind, gentle smile. Maybe she's not so bad. "Alright. That gives us a good place to start." She winces. "Good might not feel like the right word. What I mean is that the timing gives us a good place to start—when you moved here. You said in the email that you'd been having bad dreams?"

Another deep breath. It isn't exactly my favorite topic of conversation and I feel on edge after being at the police station. I run my hands over my hair and say, "Yeah, it's been scary. Thanks again. You know, for fitting me in on such short notice.

The therapist, Marie, shrugs. "There's the mixed blessing of someone canceling. I worry about them but it allows me to see someone else to worry about." Another tentative smile. "Tell me more about the dreams, and why they're so scary."

I struggle to find the words. It's really hard sometimes to say what you're feeling. It means you have to give it a name. Like naming the monster who lives under your bed. They become infinitely more familiar after that. That's why I have a hard time saying it out loud. The worst part is that this monster has an actual name, and I was too much of a chicken shit to report it. "I think... I think I was attacked. By a man. I remember being choked. But that's it. I started having dreams about it and then I had some kind of attack, and it felt like more than a dream. It was like I remembered something that actually happened to me. Is that possible?"

"Hmm. Well, we spoke briefly about the attack you had in the email you sent. I see that a lot in patients with extreme anxiety and PTSD. Are you familiar with PTSD?"

I nod. "A cousin of a friend was in Afghanistan. He came back, you know, not exactly in the best place emotionally."

"That's not surprising. The level of trauma that a lot of PTSD sufferers feel causes them so much stress that it can make their personality different. They might be more irritable than normal. It's common to self medicate as well."

I picture the flask and the pills as Marie continues. "Of course, all people are different. But it's common for PTSD victims to have panic attacks. I see it all the time. They're usually caused by having some sort of memory related to the trauma being triggered. And these attacks can be terrible. It can feel like you're losing your mind, and it can take a bit of time to come down from it. Did it feel like that when it happened to you?"

Marie takes a long drink of her tea. She has bags under her eyes and is prematurely graying at her roots. I could never be a therapist in a million years. I have enough problems of my own, and she looks like she takes other people's issues home with her. I eye her up and down and finally say, "Yeah. It was terrifying. I'm fucking lucky, though. I've got a best friend who came over and helped right away. And another friend who checked in. Well she's more of an—I don't know. Anyway, it helped, but it did take a day or two to feel even a little bit calmer."

Marie raises her eyebrow. "One friend and an 'I don't know.' Is this someone you don't like?"

"Not at all. She's… the second reason I'm here, besides the dreams. I don't know where to fit the feelings I have for her next to the feelings I have about whatever the hell is wrong with me. I've never been able to just come out and say how I feel because then, there it is. I've said it and I can't take it back. And *then*, I've forced her to try to figure out a way to fit that next to my issues and our friendship. Doesn't feel fair to her, and it just feels fucked up."

Marie nods. "Maybe it's not fair to *you* to keep it inside. You've been having dreams that make you believe you were the victim of an attack that you don't remember. It's led to issues with anxiety and intrusive thoughts. You have feelings for a friend of yours, which I also want to talk about when you're ready. I can definitely see how that could feel like a burden for you."

"I want to tell her so bad. I can't stop thinking about her, and any time I have a good dream, it's about her. Her name's Ashlin and we work together. She's one of the first people I met here who saw me for who I was. Used my pronouns, and treated me like a human. Not some fucking broken doll with a missing head. I want to be with her so badly but then she has to take on my problems, too. Plus, I don't even know what the fuck happened. Or if it happened. I obviously got away if it did. These dreams are just so vivid, and I have these same dreams over and over, I thought maybe it really could have happened. And if it did, how do I overcome that, when all I have are dreams about it? I know who it is, but I'm not ready to talk about it yet."

"If you think you may have been raped, I believe you. And I'm sorry. We can dive into that more when you're comfortable. Just say the word. Can I ask a question and make a couple of comments?"

When I don't say anything, Marie keeps going. "First of all, is it important to you to know what happened to you? To know the specifics? And go to the police and tell your story? Or can you be content with moving on and leaving it a mystery?"

I shake my head. Hell no. "No, I need to know what happened to me. For my own sake, obviously. But also, I don't want to be messed up like this forever. I want to be able to make someone else happy. I want to make Ashlin happy. But that means I have to make myself happy first. She deserves a better me."

Marie gives me a look of disapproval, like Mama does when I don't ask for seconds. "That's good to hear that you want to heal. But, you aren't messed up. You've had some negative experiences. Coming out as gay and nonbinary can be scary. You may have been attacked, which is a lot to work through, but you can't know whether or not you can make Ashlin happy without asking her opinion. It's possible you already do, as you are. People in the midst of healing deserve love, too."

My stomach flutters at the thought, and something clicks inside of my mind. The thought that I make Ashlin happy makes me feel like I can do this with my support team, and therapy. Like I can find a way to heal. Or come close to it. I'll do my best, anyway.

"We'll come back to Ashlin at our next appointment if that's okay. For now, my suggestion is to first, follow up with the police about what could have happened. If a crime was committed I'm obligated to report, but if you aren't one hundred percent sure... Who knows? The cops might be able to help. My second suggestion?"

My breath catches in my throat. The first suggestion feels overwhelming enough that I dread the second one before she even says it.

"My second suggestion is to think about all this before our next appointment, which I hope you decide to make. Are you afraid of telling Ashlin the truth just because she might not be interested, or does being vulnerable feel too difficult?"

***

Later, I spend an hour or so lying on my couch, passing the stress ball from Marie back and forth between my hands, periodically giving it a squeeze. I feel better after talking about my likely assault for some strange reason. I've spent weeks thinking about these goddamn dreams, and when I realized what they could mean, and disclosing to the cops still seems terrifying. Plus, if I tell the cops, they'll want some sort of sketch of what he looks like, and that's a no go currently. I'm too scared. Hence, the stress ball on the couch.

Why? Why me? Why would he do that to me? I try to be a good person. Not cause any waves. Alright, fine. I do get in people's faces about my pronouns sometimes, but it's a sensitive subject. And it's 2021 for fuck's sake. I still haven't even told her that it was him. I pass the ball back and forth, and wonder what consequences that conversation would have. All I know is, things would never be the same again. She would find out the worst news of her life, and she would also find out I've been keeping it from her.

My friends have been there for me the whole time. Rosa took notes on her phone about the suggestions from the therapist I told her about because my memory is shit lately, and I wanted it written down before I forgot. Ashlin held my hand after I got back from the appointment when I told her and Rosa about it. Just like in my dreams, her hand was so soft, and warm, and filled me with more comfort than any pills or drinks ever had.

I take a deep breath. I'm gonna do it. Screw it. I'm gonna do it.

This could ruin everything. It probably will. Even if I never said anything about my feelings, we're at least friends. But if I do say something, and Ashlin doesn't feel that way about me, which is likely because she's only ever dated men and never once mentioned a girl crush, she might be weirded out and never want to speak to me again. There's also the chance she could be into other sorts of people and just not feel comfortable saying that, or doesn't know it herself yet. All choices considered, if this goes tits up, the occasional platonic hand-holding from her is infinitely better than permanent silence about how I feel.

I open my text chain with Ashlin, my fingers shaking the entire time. If I had a pill, I'd pop it, but I promised Marie I'd try to cool it. Marie was hesitant to recommend prescribed medication for now because of my issues with substances, and I didn't want them anyway, but I made a standing weekly appointment. Had to start somewhere. And maybe this would give me the courage to come clean about my other secrets.

Taking a deep breath, I start to type, which results in several edits. Eventually, I hit send, biting my lip and closing my eyes. I'd written:

I need to talk to you about something. For a while, I've been feeling things that I've only recently made sense of.

Kind of a lie on my end, but I want to soften the blow.

I don't want to say this over text, but I don't know if I can say it out loud. If I wait to say it out loud, I'm scared I might never say it. I like you. I never stop thinking about you, and I just wanted you to know that.

I wait. Five minutes pass. Then thirty. Then an hour. Two hours. I'm starting to freak out that Ashlin's grossed out or trying to find a way to let me down easily. Maybe she's mad I said it over text and not in person, but that doesn't seem like her. I rattle out another text.

Are you okay? You might be at work, it's alright. Listen, I know that was a lot. Just think about what I said. Sorry. Take your time. *GIF of Samuel L. Jackson saying Tick Tock Motherfucker* Just kidding. That was awkward. Shit. Anyway... let me know how you are.

Why am I the way that I am? I mentally chide myself for not socializing more because it's biting me in the ass.

Another hour passes and still nothing.

Chapter 19

Rosa

Same Day

My email alerts me that I've got a new message.

Rosa, please come into my office at your earliest convenience. Thanks, Bill.

He does that a lot. Rather than stepping out of his office to ask me a question really quick, or ask it in the email itself, it's yet another fucking thing cluttering up my inbox.

I rub my eyes and yawn. The past few nights had been filled with restlessness and unwelcome thoughts. I've been wondering the same things I know Dannie has. Who would do this to Dannie? And why? I decide that my *earliest convenience* is not right this second.

After another quick internet search about missing women and keychains, I set my Google Chat to *away* and grab my purse. I'm craving some fresh air, so I signal to Evan that I'm stepping away and wink. He nods, and I know he'll cover for me if anyone asks. Then his eyes grow large and his fingers fly over his keyboard as he pretends to type a memo. He averts his gaze when he sees a supervisor walk past.

It's a decent-sized building, with several offices, an employee lounge, and a receptionist area at the front. My desk is a cubicle amongst others behind the reception area, so I walk past some coworkers and wave to a few. As I'm leaving, I text Dannie. Dannie's hanging around their apartment, waiting to hear back from Ashlin about something. Seems like a good excuse to meet up for a quick bite, especially after working through my lunch.

I skipped breakfast too while dealing with what felt like a month's worth of family drama on the phone. Tía's still not speaking to Marco, Mama's trying to get her sister-in-law to live in this century in regards to her son's sexuality, and one of my little sisters got fired for being late too many times. Here I am taking care of my family's shit. Again. Seeing Dannie would feel like a relief in comparison, current circumstances aside.

Instead of heading into Flora's, we grab a hotdog from a street vendor outside of Wrigley Field and sit on a bench.

Mouth full of mustard and relish, I say, "Still trying to get a hold of Ashlin?"

Dannie looks up from their phone sheepishly. They take a small bite. They haven't been eating much lately, and I know I need to bring it up at some point. I'm worried that telling them not to self-medicate is gonna lead to other bad habits. They catch my stare and take another bite. "Yeah, it's been a couple of hours and she's not answering."

"Is it an emergency? You lose your favorite Doc Martens? I can guarantee Ashlin's not wearing them." I chew and swallow, already done with the hotdog. I lean my head back against the high backed bench and soak in the Chicago afternoon sunshine. The sky's nearly free of clouds, and I smile as I close my eyes, and try to pretend that my life's a lot simpler than it is.

"My fucking Doc Martens. Of course not. I'd never lose my Docs. I told her how I felt."

My eyes widen and I sit up. Screw it, this was better than the gorgeous late spring sunshine. I never thought Dannie would tell Ashlin. Not that I don't have any faith in Dannie. I have *too* much faith, and I know that they'd do anything they could to minimize the risk of making any waves with a friend.

"And she didn't say anything?"

"Not yet," Dannie says. "She could be just thinking about it. Obviously, it's a ton of info to just drop on someone. But still. It's not like her to go hours without responding to a text. Her Google Chat's set to *away*, and she's supposed to be working today."

"Shit. I just got done dealing with family stuff this morning, and now Ashlin's on the lam."

"On the lam. It's not like she robbed a bank."

"You don't know that. Maybe she couldn't get a deal on the latest Gucci bag."

Dannie rolls their eyes, and then meets mine. They're tearless but filled with sad exhaustion. "I don't know what to do. This is all too much." Their eyes hold something else, another emotion, but for once, I can't tell what it is.

"Maybe she's working, and just turned off her chat. We can check there. Bill's in a mood and I am too. Marco's using again."

"I'm sorry. I haven't been texting him."

I pat Dannie's knee. "I know, love. He said. And he knows damn well not to lie to me at this point. This time it got so bad that Tony got hurt. Marco, he…" I bury my head in my hands, and a tear slips through my fingers. I can barely say it. "He hurt Tony."

Dannie sits up straighter. "What? Hurt him how?"

I gulp and say, "They got into a fight. Not a physical one at first, just normal 'couple' types of things. Who was supposed to do the grocery shopping and all that. Marco's been doing well, trying not to use, but the initial detox makes him agitated. It makes his PTSD flare up. I guess after the argument about shopping, Tony was just making conversation at dinner and asked about the family. He'd heard from Mama who heard from Ana about my display at Flora's." Dannie rolls their eyes and mouths, *Of course.* I continue, "So, obviously, Eric came up, and Marco lost it."

"Jesus, I'm sorry. Poor Tony. Well, he's not the greatest guy. He's actually kind of the worst. But poor Marco."

"Poor Marco indeed, Dan. You want to know the worst part? Even worse than Tony ending up with a black eye and broken nose, and the goddamn domestic charge on Marco's record now?" I pause and put my head back in my hands, speaking through the gaps in my fingers. "He told Tony something none of us ever knew. You know how Marco was honorably discharged?"

"Yeah, he was having mood issues starting and they wanted to cut it off at the pass."

I sigh. "He got outed to one of his buddies and the buddy went AWOL. The higher-ups found a note. No one knows what happened. The family and military police eventually stopped looking." I knew this would break Dannie's heart, and I hate myself for bringing it up. Being outed is such a shitty thing. But my heart feels so heavy and it all comes spilling out.

They wipe a tear away from their cheek. "Oh my God, that's fucking terrible. I can't imagine being outed before you're ready, especially in a place like that."

"You know who outed him?" I can feel ringing in my ears, and my heart's beating faster and faster by the second. "His other buddy. His Sergeant." Dannie shakes their head. She knows enough about Marco's history to know exactly who I mean.

I say his name anyway. "Eric."

"Goddamnit." Dannie pounds their fist against the bench. "I hate him so much." Their voice quavers and they take a swig from their flask hidden in the large pocket of her baggy jeans, followed by a small pill. I'd let them have this one. I know how much Eric gets under their skin.

I don't say anything at first. I don't have the energy. Watching them swallow a pill because of something I said is unbearable. Finally, after a minute or so, I say, "Eric did this. He ruined Marco's life, and I don't know how to process that. Shit. Alright, let's focus on Ashlin, because I can't do more family drama today. I'm gonna take Marco to a meeting tonight since he's staying with me while he's out on bail. Right now, let's find your girl."

***

Ashlin, I want to reiterate what I said earlier. You are one of the *best* agents on the team, and your star shines brighter here year by year. That being said, I'm disappointed at your lack of regard for professionalism and the privacy of the owner. Consider this a warning and do *not* let it happen again. Maybe it's best if you and Dannie take a break from working together. Cheri.

That's the print out Kim hands to Dannie. Dannie's face falls, and I cringe after I pry it from their hands and read it. Apparently, Ashlin mentioned the keychains. That doesn't seem like her, but maybe Cheri found out somehow and Ashlin didn't want to risk her job by lying.

Kim liked just about everyone, but especially Dannie. She always has a smile that seems specifically for them. Looking back toward Cheri's office, she waves us over. Her voice shakes, and she says, "I made these just for you, sweetie. You can have one too, hon," directing that last bit at me. Kim lifts the lid off the tupperware, and the smell makes my toes curl.

We both take one. With a mouth full of chocolate chip cookies, Dannie says, "Oh sweet Jesus. This is amazing." They swallow. "Thanks. I mean it. I wish my mom had been like you."

Kim smiles and waves her off, her eyes glossed with tears, then takes another glance at Cheri's office and gives Dannie the print out. After we read it, Kim says, "Ashlin's not here but if you want to see Cheri, she's in a meeting with a client. Maybe ten minutes?"

"Sounds good," Dannie says, voice clipped with annoyance, and we go to wait in Ashlin's office. We sit next to each other in the chairs usually saved for clients. I don't feel like getting into it with Cheri in the reception area where more people can hear. Because if she calls Dannie out, we *will* get into it.

I'm worried about Ashlin, too. Usually, if she's not answering texts, she's busy with a work issue. But she's probably okay. Maybe a family emergency, or she's busy burning Prince Eric's possessions. Lost her phone charger. Just doesn't want to answer. It could be any number of things.

I bite my lip and look at Dannie. Dannie's looking at their shoes, tapping their left foot. After a few failed attempts at speech, I finally say, "Dannie, listen—"

Dannie's head shoots up and they roll their eyes. "What did I do?" I shrink back and avert my gaze. I probably shouldn't even say anything at all.

Dannie winces. "Sorry. You know I'm just having a bad day. I don't want to take it out on you. What were you gonna say?"

"That I'm proud of you for telling Ashlin how you felt. That's all. And I'm sure she's just—"

The stomp of designer boots stops me in my tracks. Cheri's form fills the door with a huge shadow, like a fucking dementor from Harry Potter. "Can we talk in here?" Her tone is brusque, and she glances at her watch as she shuts the door.

Dannie's face looks bewildered and I bite the inside of my cheek, trying to keep my mouth shut. Dannie says, "Yeah sure. Have a—"

Cheri plops into Ashlin's chair.

"—seat," Their voice is quiet and they look at their fingernails, pretending to inspect their latest nail biting session. We'd already seen the email. Is this about the damn keychains? Was it that big of a deal?

Her eyebrows shoot up when Dannie mentions they've seen it already, but she lowers them and says, "Look, you and Ashlin are the best I have. She's maybe not the most seasoned agent here, but she closes deals. And

Dannie… I love your work and I don't want to have to go elsewhere for a photographer. Though it would be easy to find someone trainable."

I see Dannie smile sarcastically. "I'm sure," is all they say.

"So, here's what we're going to do. We're going to keep this as contained as possible. The keychains bullshit. No one outside of this office. I know it's not like you took the Crown Jewels, but that's not the reputation I want the office to have. Or the two of you, for that matter."

Cheri's gaze softens, and she offers them a weak smile. "Look, about the email. I wrote it when I was mad. I don't want to keep you here now. I know it's your day off, and you have three shoots tomorrow. Just make sure you don't let this happen again. And for God's sake, forget the keychains, okay? Leave them here in the office the next time you have them on you. The owner's one of those people, kind of weird. Probably just forgot they were in there for a while until recently. I personally don't know how you could forget you put keychains in an air vent, but different strokes, as they say. Now, go on. Have a young, carefree day before you're a grumpy old hag like me. I really am sorry about the email."

Dannie smirks and salutes as they stand up. I'm just glad the tension's gone. It's the last thing we need right now.

"Thanks," Dannie says.

"Don't thank me. Thank Ashlin. She emailed me yesterday, after coming clean to me about the keychains when the owner called to berate me, and insisted that we meet to smooth things over." *Insisted* was a little sharper than necessary. "Luckily, you showed up anyway. Ashlin's a good friend. She only told me about it in case the owner found out on his own, but she cares about you."

I look at Dannie, their jaw falling down and eyes desperate. As we leave, I realize that the two of us are falling into the eye of a massive storm and I don't know how to stop it.

"Yeah, she really does," Dannie mumbles.

Him

May 2021

My hand is still pulsing after slapping her. It felt complete, like my hand belonged on her cheek, and had for some time. She's the most beautiful thing I've ever dated, so why is she so closed off lately? Why can't she just let us have a normal relationship? That's all I ever wanted, despite how things might have started.

It's her closeness to Dannie. I'm not a moron. I can tell from the way that they look at each other how they feel. I know when Ashlin is texting them because her face lights up, and her whole body softens. I don't know whether she's a lesbian or not. Maybe she's bi, and it's me who's just unwanted, lacking in some way. I've certainly made my fair share of mistakes. Who am I kidding? I'm a complete fuck up.

But if I'm going to finally get back at that bitch Dannie, I know that this is the easiest way. The last time, they'd clawed their way out of my grasp and ran off like a goddamn gazelle. They've probably only gotten more clever over the years, especially after being attacked.

But why have they never confronted me? That's their way, calling it like it is. No bullshit. If someone attacked them, they would definitely say something, especially after the way they fought back. They would definitely have told Ashlin when she met me.

They hadn't, though. Could they have forgotten? There were things I don't remember after Afghanistan. The army doctor told me it's a coping mechanism, your brain protecting itself from the memories.

I bite the inside of my cheek and think about Marco. It was a dick move to tell Kyle Marco's gay. It isn't that kind of world anymore. At least, it shouldn't be. I'm not a homophobe, not at my core. It just kind of happened when the three of us were arguing about night duties. Kyle got belligerent with Marco, Marco lunged at him, and I tried to break it up. I was his sergeant. The only reason I was even there was for training purposes. Marco took a

swing at me, I dodged it and pinned Marco's arm behind him. I said, "You don't want to do this."

I wince at the memory. What I'd whispered in Marco's ear about continuing this and me not letting him get extra video chats from his boyfriend. I'd looked past the chats before then, because I really didn't care to be honest and Marco seemed like an alright guy. It was unintentionally just loud enough for Kyle to hear. Kyle laid into Marco, laughing and calling him the f-word.

It isn't right. None of it had been. Especially what happened next. Marco's face turned a color I've never seen. It was beyond red, beyond blood, beyond any sense of reason. Kyle said it again, and Marco flew into a rage, grabbing Kyle by the neck and squeezed. Hard.

Eventually, Kyle's body gave out and we just stared at the body, and exchanged knowing glances at each other. We knew that Kyle hadn't shown up for duty. The cameras in the night guard room were broken anyway. We hadn't heard from him since morning. And I've hated myself for it ever since. Someone doesn't have a child because of us. It makes me so angry that since I got back I've spent the last several years making bad decisions, one after the other.

So now I lean against a wall a few doors away from a bank, looking at my phone. In actuality I'm watching Ashlin walk in, a huge bag slung over her shoulder with what looked like folders in it.

A couple of hours later, Ashlin walks out next to some balding, bloated old man. They shake hands, and she waits with him while he gets into an

Uber. A smile of satisfaction lights up her face. She takes her phone out of her pocket and hesitates. By this time, the hold that Dannie has on her is so strong. Maybe Ashlin's going to see them.

Once she puts her phone in her purse, she walks back in the direction she came from. I stretch my back after leaning against that brick wall and walk after her. I'm right behind her now, so close I can smell her perfume. Sweet, with a hint of orange.

I don't know where to take her. Or how. A lot more planning used to go into my hunts, but this one's admittedly a bit impulsive. I'd always done it for some sort of thrill. I got off on the memories of kicking those bitches into the river. Letting out all of my anger. But this thrilled me so much more. This was exhilaratingly personal.

Then I thought of the perfect place. I'd just spoken to the real estate agent about it over the phone yesterday, in fact. You've gotta love voice disguisers.

It takes two or three minutes but Ashlin turns around and says, "Excuse me. Are you following me? I told you to stay the hell away." Her perfectly pink lips curl into a sneer.

"Sorry." I put my hands up in a gesture of good faith. "I really just wanted to talk."

Her eyes blink a few times. "You're joking, right? You slapped me. In what universe would I want to talk to a piece of shit like you? Plus, I need to go deal with some work stuff. I had my phone on vibrate during meetings, but an owner's mad something's missing from a house. He got into it with Cheri yesterday, and I need to head in to tie up some loose ends. He's completely off his rocker." She gives me a pointed look, her eyes telling me to beat it.

The way she says that last bit worries me. How much does she know? Maybe Dannie ended up remembering, put two and two together about who the owner was and spilled the beans. Maybe not and they're mad about what happened with Ashlin and poisoned her even more against me, considering they seem to have forgotten what happened between us.

Not just the way I hurt them, but what happened when we first met. The headshots for the website. Dannie had been new to the city, and was well recommended on LinkedIn, with a degree in photography. We met up at my office, and I offered to take them out to lunch to talk about working together. After they chastised me about using the wrong pronouns. Things hadn't gone well after that point, obviously.

Still, it doesn't make sense. Nobody's contacted me. No police. No one from the agency has made me believe anything's wrong, just the missing keychains. And Dannie took the picture. I know they always work on Ashlin's properties. If they all of a sudden remembered, why not go to the cops? And what motivation would a person have for hiding such a traumatic event from someone they seem to be head over heels for?

Women have always been a mystery to me. Sneaky little things.

"Look," Ashlin says. "I reported your ass. They said they were going to come pick you up. Where have you been hiding?"

He smiles. "I've been hiding at home. Not ours. The other one."

Chapter 20

Charlie

Now

Chris strides into the precinct, arms full of case material, and I gulp. I've been at this job for close to two decades, and I'm still intimidated a bit by people like Chris. I might love the lieutenant's pay, but I like being on the ground, at the scene with Phil, getting my hands dirty. Not sitting in a room with the Feds, arguing about DNA testing. His biceps bulging under his sleeves don't help with the intimidation factor either.

He stops at the front of the lobby, his eyes full of questions, and flirts with the cop on desk duty. The cop points over toward me, and she waves goodbye to him. He winks back, with a devilish grin. I broke things off with him, for good this time, and he still manages to make me feel weak in places I shouldn't.

Chris steps up to greet me and says, "Good morning, Lieut."

"Call me Charlie for Christ's sake. 'Lieut' sounds, I don't know. Sexy somehow."

"I can see where your mind is," Chris says, his eyes looking me up and down.

"To be fair, I do make the disrespectful, misogynist assholes at my precinct call me Lieutenant."

Chris laughs. "Oh, I wouldn't expect anything less from you, my dear."

"Alright then, let's get to work."

We head into an empty meeting room that I had repurposed for the strangulation killer information. In it is a long gray table with a dozen or so chairs, and four gigantic dry erase boards. On three of them, I have photos, newspaper clippings, and I've written any relevant info I could think of in what my fellow cops call my "chicken scratch." One is left over for possible leads.

Chris eyes it over for a few minutes, and then sets the case files down on the table. When he looks back at the board, he spends a minute or two studying the side-by-side images of the victims—the *befores* and *afters*. "They were pretty."

I swallow a moment of sadness and say, "I spoke with the latest husband just about an hour ago, and he said he's willing to come meet with us and give you a replay of his statement. To see what you make of it. The missing keychain. Did the guy take it? I've been at this job seventeen years this summer, and I've never seen a signature like that. Why? Is it some kind of trophy?"

Chris holds up a hand. "Let's not get ahead of ourselves. We could be looking at that possibility. He also took the second one, but it would be helpful if we had even just one more to compare it to. One preferably with DNA." After a surprised look from me, he continues, saying, "Obviously, I don't want to be dealing with a serial. I'm just making a point. We need a definitive pattern. I want to see the husband, more than one if I can, and I want to meet with the Chief so the three of us can put our heads together."

"I don't know what's going on here. Several missing women turn up dead by a river, same MO, a few missing a keychain. It's damn spooky."

Phil walks in carrying two cups of coffee, and says, "Sorry to interrupt. But I thought you could use this." He sets them down and sticks out his hand. "Detective Phil Anders, Lieutenant Carlson's partner. She lets me hang around as a partner, anyway. I don't know if you remember me."

"Of course, man." He shakes Phil's hand. A few other detectives file in. "Why don't you all take a seat while I get started on the other board, and we can see what we're dealing with." He starts hanging up more pictures and notes when my phone rings. I can see Chris listening while he clips things up.

"What? Really? Jesus. Okay. What about the girlfriend? Seriously? Thanks for the head's up." I turn to Chris and say, "I need a few minutes to follow up on something. It's about the report on the domestic." With an annoyed look from him, I continue. "I know we have a lot going on here, but the circumstances made me feel bad, especially considering he nearly choked her."

I head back to my office, not waiting for his permission, or needing it. I grab a notepad and make a to-do list. The boyfriend's in the wind, according to the cops assigned to look for him, and no one's heard from Ashlin. I can still picture the way the poor woman's body shook as she described his hand around her neck. It was time to start asking more questions.

***

"You haven't heard anything? She hasn't called to say she was taking a sick day?"

"No, nothing. Not since before the closing she did at the Chase down the road," the frantic woman says. "It's not like her at all. I did get an email from her, but it seemed off. Not the way she usually writes."

"Mhmm." The woman is Ashlin's boss. Her name's Cheri. They transferred the call to me because I'd filed the initial report. When I first picked up the phone, she had a no-nonsense quality about her, which I like in a person. But the second Cheri mentioned Ashlin's name she became more upset. "Any recent personal issues, apart from the domestic?"

"Domestic? I don't know much about that, but Kim told me. It's a busy time of year, so Ashlin might not have wanted to bring it up if there was, or was embarrassed. I was pretty mad the other day though."

I raise my eyebrows and lift my pen to take another note. "Mad about what, ma'am?"

"She and our photographer, Dannie, they took something from a house they did a shoot at. You know, they took pictures for a listing." Cheri waits and when I remain silent, she says, "Anyway, the owner found out, and might pull the listing and move back in himself. He's been looking for tenants but he changed his mind. Just like that. He was pissed about it though. The guy's name is Vance Michaels apparently. I know it sounds crazy, but he always preferred to operate under an anonymous business entity. He came clean about the name after I told him I didn't like him swearing at me, and I was ready to call the cops in to deal with this. The house from the listing's address is 4761 Wayne Avenue, in case that's helpful."

"It is, thank you. Wait. Dannie? I know them. Okay. What'd they take? An item of value, I assume?"

"That's the thing. I've never heard of anything like it. All they took was a set of keychains." I hang up, drop my notebook back on my desk after ripping off a piece of paper, and sprint out of the precinct.

***

I stand outside, desperate for fresh air. My hand grows numb as I grip the phone, my voice raised as I say, "Ashlin. Call me back. This is serious. And do not make contact with Eric for any reason. Please call me as soon as you get this."

I fight to catch a breath and look at the next number on the sheet of paper. The person on the other end picks up immediately. They say, "Hello? Who is this?"

I say, "Lieutenant Carlson. Charlie. We spoke the other day. I'm looking for Ashlin. Well, I was looking for the boyfriend because we have a warrant for his arrest after her report. But now I can't get a hold of Ashlin either."

Dannie's voice is rushed, the sound of heaviness resonating in her throat. "I can't either. I don't know where she is and I'm seriously freaking out."

"Do you know a Vance Michaels?"

"No, why?"

"He's the owner of the house you and Ashlin did a photoshoot at. I'm wondering if he's involved somehow because of the keychains he *somehow* forgot about until now."

"That's the house," they say, sounding miles away.

"What house?" What the hell is going on?

Dannie pauses and says, "I just saw a therapist and told her I think I might have been raped. I've been seeing it more vividly in my dreams, and I'm sure that's where it was. That... It happened at that house. Shit, I think I know—"

I lose focus and close my eyes, envisioning myself wrapping them in my arms. Stroking their hair in my mind, I hold them for a minute or two, thinking about all the women lying on the riverbeds. Could Dannie have been one that got away? I realize they're saying something.

"I got lost in thought there. I'm so sorry that happened to you. I understand why you didn't bring it up when we met. It's a tough thing. Listen, swing by the precinct and give me those keychains if you still have them. I'm happy to take your report, too, if you feel more comfortable talking to me." Before I hang up I say, "And, Dannie? We'll find her. I promise."

I hear a "Charlie, wait," before the line goes dead. I would call them back, but I need to find Ashlin.

I hate making promises like that. We're technically not supposed to, but my head's spinning in circles. I have a house in town where one person was sexually asssaulted, and potential evidence from serial murders was found there. I have a missing real estate agent who listed that house, who also has a missing abusive ex-boyfriend. Then there's Vance Michaels, whoever the hell that was.

I go back in and head to my computer and type Vance Michaels in the DMV records. It immediately pulls up a photo. The man looks like he's in his thirties, and I'm struck by how handsome he is, especially his haunting blue eyes.

Him

Now

Ashlin shakily steps out of the Uber. I'm not an idiot, despite what she might think. I took a separate cab and paid cash, wearing a baseball cap and sunglasses. An overdone trope, a page out the *You* textbook, but it was better than nothing. I'd said to her hours ago, "Go into your office. Check your email. Schedule one to go out in one hour and another in two hours and three hours. Take an Uber to Wayne Avenue. Pay in cash. Don't try anything stupid."

After sitting here for almost forty-five minutes, watching from inside the house, she walks up. It reminds me of that movie I've seen a couple of times. It's actually a pretty good one. *The Green Mile*. That long walk the prisoners have to take before they meet their fate.

There weren't any surveillance cameras right outside of the agency so it had been easy enough for her to slip me the key to the house. As she comes up the short walkway, I start growing hard. This is going to make Dannie furious.

Where the fuck is Dannie? They're the key to all of this, no pun intended. They forgot about me and never reported the assault. I need to make sure that never happens. They're close to Ashlin, too close, and they've got to be in love with her or something. Who the hell knows? Dannie's also best friends with Rosa. The incident in Afghanistan has never come up. Another thing I have to make sure never happens. This is getting messier by the minute.

There are a hell of a lot of loose ends to tie up, especially with the cops looking for me.

Ashlin creeps into the house, her shaking visible from yards away. The only thing that seems to keep her from breaking my rules and sprinting out of there must be my threats about Dannie. Just a guess on my part. I told her I knew all about it, the playful flirting, the hidden feelings. That's what it's been all this time. Maybe this would be what it takes to get her to admit it. I want to hear her say it out loud, and watch her realize that she would never see Dannie again. It's going to break her. She's never going to get the chance to tell them how much she thought about them when she should have been thinking about me instead. I laugh at the thought and think about my next move.

Ashlin watches these kinds of movies all the time. She ought to know how this next part works. The camera pans from the tragic victim to the evil monster. The funny part is that they hardly ever look like monsters. I look like the handsome guy sitting next to you at the bar, which has worked in my favor so far.

She walks toward me. "Okay, look. I did what you asked. What's this all about? Our break up? Dannie?" Tears run down her cheeks, and she gulps. I glance out of the window for a moment, and she quietly reaches her hand into her purse. Thinks she's being sneaky.

I jerk my head back in her direction. "No. No! I said no fucking around!" I leap up and snatch her purse, throwing it into the corner, making her yelp.

My eyes narrow. "I know you're trying to text your girlfriend."

"They're not my girlfriend. You know that. They're my friend." She forces a laugh, even though her voice is trembling, and says, "You know how it goes, right? Things get misinterpreted. People get jealous. I think that's what happened here. I texted them a bit too much, and it seemed like something it wasn't."

"Dannie infuriates me. You know, a long time ago I got rejected by them. Before you and I started dating."

Ashlin's eyes narrow. She had no idea. But she smiles, the fakest smile I've ever seen, and she says, "Maybe we can come to some kind of arrangement. The last thing I want is to make you mad like that again."

What is she up to? "What about Dannie? You care about them."

Ashlin sighs. "I know. I lied about not liking them, okay? I do care about them that way. But they don't seem to feel the same. I wouldn't know though, I've never asked. Just like they rejected you, that's how I'm starting to feel, like there's no interest. I didn't have hope for anything between me and Dannie, I promise."

"But I've seen them. They flirt with you all the time. Are you too stupid to notice?"

"Flirting, yeah. I've noticed it a bit. But have they kissed me? Touched me like you do? No. Despite me making it pretty clear what I want."

I thrust forward and slam her against the wall. "Look, I'm not a fucking moron. What? Are you trying to appeal to my better nature? My humanity? Does it seem like I have a lot of that right now?"

More tears spill down Ashlin's cheeks and her chest heaves with sobs. She has to know that she's never going to see Dannie again. And she's never told them how she feels. Look where being afraid gets people. Poor stupid Ashlin.

"Please. I don't—I don't want to make you angry. What do you want me to do?"

A genuine smile spreads across my face. "We're going to go upstairs and have a little fun."

***

It's a risk but I drive around town, in sight of local CCTV. I need to find Dannie. They're probably still in Wrigleyville somewhere, looking for Ashlin.

I dial a number from the car. Another gamble. But the cops having the sock, and Ashlin telling them about our argument, makes me feel desperate. After the call, I drive away and pull up in front of an old apartment complex about ten minutes away. It's growing more dilapidated by the day, but not enough to warrant being labeled condemned. It's disgusting.

A few minutes later, my passenger door opens, and he gets in. I'd called him telling him I wanted to make things right, and eventually he agreed to a quick chat, *real fucking quick* as he put it, and a business transaction. I point a knife low against his side, where nobody outside of the car would be able to see it.

His voice shakes and he says, "I told you, I never wanted to see your fucking face ever again, cabrón. Put that down, really. You know I gotta pay rent." Marco hands me the bag. "But after this, I'm over it. I'm trying to be done with this shit. Get clean. No matter how much money someone offers. I'll try to see if Rosa can help me out again."

"This better be what I asked for."

"You're lucky I had some lying around. I hid them. When I came back, I set some aside. I wanted to off myself. You know why, right?" I don't answer because I *do* know why, and don't want to talk about it. Marco continues anyway. "Take one of these and it'll knock you on your ass. You're gonna need someone to drag you home. Take more than one? I don't recommend that. What the fuck do you need these for?"

"Insomnia. The other ones aren't cutting it anymore." What he doesn't know is I might need at least one of them to drag someone home.

Marco exhales. "Well, one'll do it. But don't take more than one. I don't want more blood on my hands. Even yours."

He throws the bag at me, and I say, "Get out. I never want to see you again, either."

Before I drive away, I lean back against my headrest. How many more would be enough? How many more women would make me stop hating

Dannie? There were so many, they're all starting to become merged together in my mind.

Chapter 21

Rosa

Now

D annie and I watch Charlie drop the keychains into a plastic bag with a gloved hand after she fills out Dannie's report about their assault.

"There you go," I say, glad to be done with it. The damn things had done nothing but add stress to our lives. And life was stressful enough as it was.

I'd just spent even more money on my family paying Marco's bail the other day. Now I was letting him stay with me. He's an outcast as far as our family was concerned, a massive disappointment, and didn't have anywhere else to go. He could go to rehab but that was more money I don't have. He could stay in a shelter, but I don't trust he wouldn't start using again there.

He could start over at my apartment, and it was the best I could do under the circumstances.

Charlie smiles and takes a deep breath. "You two have no idea how much this helps. Might not be any DNA on them, but you never know. They could end up being helpful."

"I hope so," I say. "Thanks for… doing what you do, and all that."

Dannie remains silent, their eyes mostly cast on the ground, but keep darting up to Charlie. I've never seen them more afraid in their life. I know the whole thing is eating away at them, Ashlin being missing, the triggering memories of the house. Dannie hadn't wanted to turn the keychains in. They seem to give Dannie an unconventional lack of control. We might not be able to find Prince Eric—Charlie's staying mum on some of the assault case details because she said they might be related to another ongoing case—but if Dannie keeps the keychains, they're taking something important from him. That had to feel good, and worse now that they have to give them up.

Charlie heads back inside, leaving us out here, unsure where to go now. I look at Dannie and say, "What now, love?"

Dannie shrugs. "I'm furious at myself, and I'm scared."

"Why? You did a brave thing, telling your story. Charlie will make sure nothing happens to you."

"That's not—I'm just going back to my apartment to wait. We already tried everywhere we could think of. Maybe Ash is just mad or something and she'll text me back later."

I wrap Dannie in a long, tight hug, and after a few moments Dannie wraps their arms around my neck and lays their head on my shoulder. I can feel my neck getting damp. "I'm frightened," they say.

"I know. She's probably—" I don't get to finish my sentence because Charlie comes back out, her breath ragged.

She glances around as if to make sure no one's watching us and says, "Look, I shouldn't even tell you this. I could get major shit for it. But I want you to find Ashlin. I did some digging into the owner of that house earlier. I just wanted to tell you. His name is Vance Michaels. You all sure you don't know anyone by that name?" We both shake our heads. Charlie continues, "It's the house. All of this started with that house on Wayne Ave. Just be careful, and by no means go there unless I tell you to, alright? Vance could be the one behind the murders we're looking into, and he could be holed up there."

Dannie's eyes widen. "I gotta go, Rosa. Thanks, Lieutenant." Charlie goes back inside, her feet trudging with fatigue.

Dannie sprints off right away, once Charlie was out of eyesight, and I try to keep up with them, my breath stuck in my lungs as I find myself cursing my savior complex.

***

I am way too out of shape for this. I finally caught up with Dannie. Morning yoga was one thing. Full on sprinting's not my cup of tea. "Where the hell are you going?"

"Just back to the apartment. I want to hurry back in case she shows up there."

My ass they are. "We've been friends for a long time. I know when you're full of shit. I can tell you're hiding something from me. We've spent just about our whole lives telling each other everything. And now you've got something in that brain of yours that you don't trust me with."

"It's not that I don't trust you. I'm scared out of my mind that I won't be able to get to Ash in time. I'm not full of shit, I just want to be ready. She could stop by at any time."

My eyes narrow. Another lie. But I know when Dannie can't be persuaded. "Alright. But damn, it's not gonna be in the next three seconds, is it? Take a deep breath." I put my hand on Dannie's cheek, the warmth from the exertion giving the midday sun a run for its money.

"I can't. I can't breathe until I know where she is. Just let me head home. I'll text you if I hear anything."

"Fine, but please. Do not go to that fucking house, and text me if you leave the apartment or hear anything."

"Pinkie promise, and all that shit," Dannie says, their eyes darting around.

"Okay, go, go. Just keep me posted." I know they're still lying, but I feel helpless, weighed down and unable to follow them. I make sure Find My Friend is turned on and watch them run off. I add Charlie's number to my speed dial and hope to hell that the house isn't where Ashlin is. Her location is turned off. I swear to God.

***

I text Dannie an hour later.

Anything?

No answer. I try to tell myself that Dannie's probably drinking or went out again to check Ashlin's apartment. I wait another hour and try again.

Dannie, where you at? Have you heard anything? Call me.

Why hadn't I gone with them? I knew exactly where they were going, and I failed them. Maybe I'm so burned out from the situation with Marco I wasn't thinking clearly. Who the hell am I if I'm not protecting someone?

Still no response. I look at the clock and it's been almost two and a half hours since my first text. It's getting close to dinner time. First Ashlin, now Dannie. What the fuck is going on? I call Dannie's third emergency contact, besides me and Ashlin—Dannie's next door neighbor. She's an adorable, sweet old lady that brings Dannie a casserole each Sunday. Helen says she's been home all day, and hasn't heard from them or heard them come back inside.

Now, I'm really freaking out. This isn't *Broadchurch*. It isn't a documentary on Netflix. This is happening right now, in real time, and it isn't entertaining in the least. I know I have another call to make.

Chapter 22

Dannie

Now

I love Rosa. She's my best friend in the whole world. But she's wrong this time, and so is Charlie. I have to go to the house. It's the only place in the world I can go. The only place my body calls me to, toward Ash and the place that holds traumatic memories. Like Charlie said, the whole mystery started there, and I have a feeling that's where it's going to end.

I have to go to Wayne Avenue.

So, I run. It stings, but I run until my lungs feel like they're going to collapse and my legs have no energy left. Maybe there was something to Rosa's suggestion of a daily walk after all. Eventually, I make my way there, and I'm standing out front, drenched in sweat, and soaking up all the horrors that happened to me in this house, as they barrage me with sudden clarity.

My body fights against going inside. It's the last place on Earth I want to be, but my body's beginning to remember. It's hard to put into coherent thought, the way your body can remember a trauma long after it's happened and your mind struggles to accept it as truth. But now I remember the fear, the pain, the questions of whether or not I was going to live. I can feel the way he touched me, the way he hurt me as if it happened yesterday. The longer I stare at the house, the more I remember those eyes looming over me.

They were bright blue and full of hatred. His hair flopped over his forehead, which I now know is normally made neater by excessive amounts of styling product. He'd looked deranged, not at all like the man I'd come to know later, who always looked ready to go to a business meeting. That day, he was a monster. And now I know he still is.

I never want to look at him again. The thought makes me sick to my stomach, and I choke back rising vomit. But I know that if I don't go face this *now*, face him, he might be doing the same things to Ash that he did to me, if he hadn't already. I gather up whatever strength I have left, run up the front walkway to the door, and burst inside, my breath ragged from the effort.

***

I inch up the stairs, and one of them creaks. I thought they fixed the stairs, thinking back to the photoshoot with Ash. Maybe we'd missed it. I can't remember. The small hope I have of finding her safe is all I can cling to right now. Ash could be up there with Eric, having God knows what done to her.

If he lays one goddamn finger on her…

He must not have heard the creak because I can hear him talking, his voice dripping with condescension like always. I strain to hear, as I approach the door. It's the bedroom, the horrible one. The one that made me the way that I am, shrunken and hollow, hiding inside my own body. My mind repels against nearing closer, and my body wrestles with my mind, telling me not to open the door. The logical part of me, whatever is left of it, knows I have to get close enough to figure out what is going on and come up with some kind of plan.

I hear him say, "Oh this is just perfect." He laughs, the noise coming out deranged and terrifying. A memory of that laugh burrows into my mind, and I fight back a hailstorm of emotional pain.

Ash must be tied up and gagged in the bed upstairs. I can hear her thrashing around and trying to scream. It's all coming back to me, wave upon wave of horror and pain and humiliation, but I press on, getting closer to the door by the second, hoping there aren't any more creaky floorboards.

Does he have a weapon of some kind? I have no way of knowing so I have to play it safe. Finally, I'm at the door. It's shut, but I press my ear up against it.

Ash thrashes on the bed and yells, the words muffled by the gag. I can hear those four bed posts being strained against and I close my eyes. A tear rolls down my cheek, and my lip trembles. The memories assault me. I need to keep my breathing under control, keep it steady and even, not the broken mess that's trying to claw its way out.

I picture her in the same state I'd been in when Eric did this to me years ago, her chest exposed and trembling. Then I stop. What's perfect? He said something was *just perfect*.

I think I hear Ash mumble something that sounds like *asshole*. Eric growls, saying, "Tell me your passcode. I tried guessing, but we never had that kind of relationship, did we? I bet Dannie knows it."

I don't, but I wonder what it is that he is so anxious to see on her phone.

"Kuh tuh yuh pahhcuh wheh yuh hah mm gah."

"Fine. Jesus. Here, you bitch." I can hear him take off her gag, and my hands shake, pulse pounding. He keeps on and says. "Just tell me the goddamn password. Screaming is not going to do you, or Dannie, any favors."

Ash doesn't say anything, and then she *does* scream, and he slaps her. What's he doing? When will I have the strength to walk in? To save the person I need and face the monster that I now know ruined so many people's lives, including my own?

"Tell me your passcode," he says, I imagine through gritted teeth. Each word is a furious exclamation.

Ash's voice shakes, and she says, "One. One."

I put my hand on the doorknob, and it burns in my hands. Whatever Eric has planned cannot be good. My heart races uncontrollably, and I force myself to turn the handle, to somehow have the strength.

"Okay, fine. One. One. One. Nine. Eight. Nine." She writhes against the restraints, snarling at him. It's so loud that she sounds like a tiger waiting to be fed. I stifle a sob. There's no way. No way in hell. I had no idea.

"That's not your birthday. Or mine. Usually it's a birthday, or anniversary. So whose is it?"

I heard Eric howl, and I run in, thankful he'd been stupid enough to leave the door unlocked. He's clutching his finger, which was bleeding. My eyes dart to Ash, her lips covered in blood. We hold each other's gaze, frozen in time.

Eric looks up and sighs, wincing in pain. He puts the gag back in. "Good. Dannie's here. Saves me a step, I guess." He turns his attention back to Ash. "You're getting to be a problem. I was just going to tell you what your texts said. If you want to hear them. I'm assuming Dannie does, too?" It's less a question than a challenge.

I approach the bed and Eric holds up his hand. "Hold on, let me open these up. I only saw the preview and it was super cute. Want to hear it?"

Ash continues fighting the ties around her wrists and legs, thrashing around like she was possessed. "Nuh. Nuh duh. Stuh ih."

Eric looks down at the phone. I inch closer to the bed, since his eyes are drilled into the screen. He says, "Sounds like a no, but I'm feeling a bit playful. Let's see…" His eyes scan the text. "What do you know? It's from Dannie."

She sobs through her gag he made from her shirt, which now looks soaked. She tilts her head back and tries to scream, but it comes out in desperate sobs. Her eyes plead, begging him not to read it. I would give anything to run over, cover her up, give her more dignity than Eric had given me all those years ago. But I don't want to make things worse. At least I'm here now.

My body quakes with fear as Eric opens his mouth. This is it. This is what I've waited years to say, and Eric was stealing my chance. This psycho is going to say it for me.

"Alright, gonna do my best Dans impression." He clears his throat and affects an overly dramatic female voice, which I know damn well is a personal jab. "'I need to talk to you about something.' Ooh, sounds like hot goss."

I give him a death stare as he keeps going. "'For a while, I've been feeling things that I've only recently made sense of. I don't want to say this over text, but I don't know if I can say it out loud.' Jesus Christ, this is worse than Nicholas Sparks."

I look at Ash, who is staring at Eric. Her eyes widen and finally, the tears stop falling. She's completely still, and completely quiet.

Female voice, "'If I wait to say it out loud, I'm scared I might never say it.' Wonder what they have to say."

She makes an attempt at a roar. "Stuh!"

"What?" he asks, cupping his hand over his ear. He pulls down the gag.

"I said stop. Please. This isn't fair."

I choke back sobs and wish I had the strength to run over to her. It has only allowed me in the room so far, and I'm weighing my options. She looks so scared, and as he puts the gag back in, the tears resume their long journey down her cheeks and onto the shred of blouse in her mouth. To hell with it, I decide to run over and rip it out as he's putting it in. Fuck him and fuck the mouth gag.

"Don't be an idiot, Dannie." He slams me against the ground, my elbow clashing against the hard floor. After seeing I'm down, he continues to read, "'If I wait to say it out loud, I'm scared I might never say it. I like you. I never stop thinking about you, and I just wanted you to know that.' Aww. They just want you to know."

Ash wails, and yanks her right arm back and forth, making the tie move with it and the bed shake. I lie cowering on the floor. I want to untie her, to save her and run out of the room with her and never look back, but I'm still afraid of what Eric might do. I settle for saying, "Let her go, Eric. Just leave this between the two of us. You can do whatever sick thing you want to me. Just let her go." I stumble over to him and hit him as hard as I can on the chest, but he seems unfazed, grabbing my arm and pinning me to him.

"Blah blah blah. That lame GIF with Samuel L. Jackson that must be something you would normally find funny. Yes, Dannie. This is awkward, to answer your question in the text." He lets me go, shoving me against the ground again, and climbs on top of Ash. She flinches as he pushes himself against her.

I get up, strength coming from I don't know where, and jump on his back. Like hell is he going to hurt her even more. Or me, for that matter.

I wrestle with him, struggling to push him off, but I know I'm losing. I'm exhausted. Tired of hiding, and fighting, but right now I'm *very* tired of Eric and I continue to cling to him as he maintains a grip on Ash's phone.

He shakes me off. I land on the ground again with a thud. He says, "She just wants to make sure you're okay. Isn't that sad? I think it is."

How dare he? How dare he take my feelings for her, after he's taken so much from me already, and turn them into a sick game. He's fucking laughing. Before he can see it coming, I jump up and kick him between the legs, emboldened by the need to save Ash.

"I've got this, Ash. You're going to be okay."

He yelps and falls over, clutching his wounded erection. He gets up, grimacing and says, "You'd better feel lucky that I still want to fuck you,

Ashlin. To piss off dear Dannie." His voice is weaker than usual, but still drips with malice.

I deal the final blow, one that I might not ever have the chance to make again. I whisper, "I remember now, *Prince Eric.*" I say the last part with his usual level of condescension, remembering Rosa's nickname for him. "Rosa calls you that behind your back. You've got to know why. Because you're spoiled, demanding. You think you're entitled to anything you lay your goddamn hideous eyes on. And it's a joke to us. You're a joke."

Ash shakes the bedposts as hard as she can. She drops back into stillness, drenched with sweat. I know this might be the last time I ever see her, and that text made it all worse. It would be burned in our minds forever. Or for however much time we have left. *I'm scared I might never say it.* It's seared in my mind, too. I don't know what will happen next. I think he's going to kill me, but he took everything from me, and I'm quaking with anger.

I hate this. Not so much the fact that I might die as the thought that I had been so weak, and so scared—that I never told Ash how I felt before this whole mess. I would never feel Ash's touch, her kiss, outside of my dreams.

Maybe we could have had a life, at the very least continuing our friendship. Ash would have done whatever she could to help me get well, I know that much. We'd be in it together for the long haul after going through something like this together. But then I let out a feeble laugh. There's no way we're going to make it out alive.

I close my eyes. I can still feel him lying on top of me all those years ago, blue eyes sparkling with frightening amusement, the way he felt as he pushed himself inside me, his hands around my neck. I fall to the ground, gasping for air, bringing my own hands to my throat.

I'm able to manage a glance at Ash. I know she feels weak and she's finding it hard to stay awake. She's exhausted from the screaming and thrashing, and the emotions that filled the entire room like a blazing fire.

We're both just exhausted. So I keep thinking. There must be a way to save her, to save us.

I could spend time thinking about what might have been. Ash and I, together. In love in the open. Exchanging kisses whenever we wanted to. Rosa rolling her eyes and telling us to get a room, all the while smiling. Goddamnit. The way her kisses would have felt, her arms wrapped around my neck.

But I don't have time to let my mind go there, so before it did I stopped myself. In the hellscape we're currently in, she's drifting off to sleep, lying in the disgusting bed he'd tied her up in.

Slam.

I shoot up, as much as I can given the panic that's setting in. He's still on the ground after I kicked him. His fist slams against the ground over and over again. With each one, my heart thuds. So far, he'd tied Ash up and mocked her, mocked me and my love for her. What did this angry thudding mean for us now?

He gets up and ungags her, waking her from her sleep, bringing her back to the real nightmare. "I'm tired of dealing with this thing. Just be quiet, and stay awake. Both of you. We aren't done here."

He paces around the chair he sat in earlier. Ash's eyes flick back and forth, watching him circle it. She periodically looks at me, and Eric watches us both.

"Listen. I'm really fucking pissed." He holds up a hand. "Whatever. I don't know what to do with this." He gestures as if to mean, what? The general situation? His feelings about losing his girlfriend? He sucks on his injured finger and limps as he continues walking.

"What's this all about?" I ask. "You didn't like me rejecting you after the job interview so you attacked me? I'm guessing you started dating Ash to get back at me. You don't like my feelings for her, and you're mad about the breakup. But attacking us? This makes no sense."

"It does to me. And that's what matters."

"Well, maybe I can help somehow," I say.

"And how the fuck can you do that?"

"Tell me what this is about, and I can… I don't know. Maybe I know people who could help you figure this out on the down low. Cover it up. It's Chicago. No shortage of shady people."

He laughs and points at me. "You're funny. Unfortunately, there's only one person who can help me. And guess what? I found you."

Ash continues tiredly working against the restraints. "Why don't you leave them out of this?" Her voice is beginning to slur.

"Because she's the reason I'm here in the first place, Ashy. She… you wouldn't understand. Dannie was the first."

Him

Eric

July 2015

She's cute. Not normally my type, but there's something about her. A mixture of confidence and complete lack of. She's sitting across from me, me behind my desk and her in a chair in front of it. Her arms rest on her knees, but she keeps adjusting them, obviously nervous. She's a bit younger than me, a year or two out of college, and this might be her first real break into the industry. Working with us would be an asset for her career.

"Dannie Northrop. Degree in photography from UW-Mad... Portfolio looks good." I look up from the folder she brought with her. "You seem like a smart girl."

She scoffs and says, "No offense, Eric, but I'm not that much younger than you, and I'm nonbinary. They, them, theirs, not a girl, etc. Just so we're clear."

I should have been offended, but a part of me respected it. A total lack of fucks at a job interview. Knowing who she is and what she deserves. I try to be that way, self-assured, and it's an air I'm constantly putting on, but the effort is sometimes so strong, I go home and need a stiff drink or two to recover.

Growing up, I heard it all the time, especially from my mother. "Why can't you be like your father? At least he's made something of himself.

You're in school and can't even manage to get higher than a *B* minus in any of your classes."

I was aware that my dad paid a lot of my teachers off to bump my grades from *C*'s and *B*'s to at least an *A* minus., and it stung. I worked as hard as I could, but it was never enough. Today, looking at Dannie, who just schooled me about her pronouns, I wonder what her own mother was like. *Their*. Their mother. I crack my neck, the remembrances of childhood causing the beginning of a headache, and I was desperate to take one of the pills in my desk.

After high school, I joined the Marines. Did two tours in Afghanistan and made my way up to Sargeant. It wasn't easy, and I did a lot of things I'll never be able to unsee, but I was able to get a business degree and leadership experience that helped me get the job here a few years ago. After being overseas, my self-confidence was worse than ever and meeting Dannie was refreshing.

"Listen," I say, "I like you. I like your work." Looking at my watch, I add, "It's almost noon. Let's go to lunch and talk about pay and all that fun stuff." They agreed, and we got into my car, my shiny new red BMW.

That's when everything started to go wrong.

Chapter 23

Dannie

Now

"The first *what*?" Ash looks at me, her voice raised to a near yell. "The first one. The first person who had the audacity to ruin my life, apart from my mother." He shrugs and my pulse quickens. "There she was sitting in my office. Dannie. I liked the look of her, despite the godawful hair. And she honestly is a great photographer. So different from all the women I'd ever met and something drew me to that. Dannie and I had a little work chat, and I bought her a drink. I'm simple, like most men, and tried to use a pick up line. Maybe not my best one, but it was what came to mind at the time. And Dannie said, 'Hell no. That's gross, hitting on someone at a job interview.' She went to the bathroom, and it was obvious that the point was to make a phone call. I'm simple, but not stupid. When she was gone, I slipped a pill in her drink when she wasn't looking. Okay, maybe two."

"That's how I got here. You drugged me." My statements came out like questions.

Ash's voice fills up the small room. "What did they do to you? They're the best person I know. What was so awful that you turned into this monster?"

I cringe. It's going to come out now. In a way, I'm glad. I know it needs to at some point, but my cheeks flush and I feel a wave of nausea roll over me. "Stop," was all I could get out without risking throwing up everywhere.

Eric ignores me and keeps his focus on Ash. "The funny thing is, I really grew to like you, Ashlin. It was so tempting. So tempting to take it all away from Dannie and add you to my collection. But there was always something stopping me. I don't know. Call me old fashioned, but I thought maybe if we stayed together, I could feel normal and my anger would stop. Or maybe I'd get over the Dannie thing. She obviously had, or had forgotten about it altogether. So I stoked it, and stoked it, and stoked it. I stoked it until the fire grew too strong, when you started grinning from ear to ear every time Dannie texted you. I've been thinking about this moment ever since, but I knew it had to be right. Right at the point of no return, as they say. Luckily for me, I've had a lot of practice over the past several years since Dannie."

"You've done this to more than one person? Jesus Christ," I say, still glued to the ground like a submissive dog, glued by the weight of my trauma, my rejection of him, and the things it caused him to do.

"I never get rejected anymore. Until you and Dannie came along. I've worked long and hard to make sure of that since I left home," Eric says. "But I'll never be good enough for anyone. I said I 'never get rejected,' which is mostly true. But you've met my mother, Ashlin. She's a mess. Drinking was always more important than loving me, and that's all I've ever wanted. To be loved."

Eric looks around. He seems to be gathering his thoughts, and I calculate the odds of being able to get away. Can I incapacitate him long enough to untie Ash and get away?

He keeps monologuing, not seeming to know who he's even talking to anymore, dissociative. "I've been with a lot of women, but nothing meaningful. It made me feel worthwhile, useful in a strange way. Then Dannie came into my life, and it was just one more reminder that I was a piece of trash, and I'd had enough. I might have done something rash with the drugs, gambling on how to give her, but I bought some pills from an old friend to help me with some sleep issues, and the opportunity fell into my lap."

My eyes grow large with horror. I never wanted Marco involved in all this. I see Eric look at the window, and at the floor, and finally at the ceiling. He stops and stares at it. Shit. I hadn't noticed it when I burst in here. There is a small crack in the wall by where I had unscrewed the vent, and I remember that he knew we'd taken them. Cheri had mentioned it.

Eric's breath hitches, and he climbs on the bed again. Ash groans as he steps on her shins. He creeps closer to the wall and peers inside. Looking for what, I have no damn idea. After a minute or two, Eric kneels down on the bed, pulling himself closer, and strokes her cheek. He's in a trance, and she's staring back at him, her eyes welling with tears.

I kick him as hard as I can in his lower back.

No way can I let him do to Ash what he did to me. All of a sudden, he grabs my neck with one hand, making it hard to breathe. Slowly, his other hand moves down Ash's neck and chest, and he caresses one of her breasts. Each one of us in the palm of his hand, like ragdolls. He drops me, and I fight for air.

She rattles the restraints as he pushes his mouth against hers. He slips his tongue inside her mouth and she grimaces, crying even harder. I see him put something into her mouth, and jam her mouth closed so she's forced to swallow it eventually. "Your turn, Dannie." He holds up another one, and dangles it in front of me just like the keychains.

I suppress bile. How can he do this to us? Is he just another fragile human? I never saw him that way until now. If anything he'd been arrogant. Now he is cruel, no longer a victim, and the monster we see in him is no longer just in my nightmares. But, perhaps, once upon a time he had been someone in need of help himself. I could feel sorry for him, even if that was true, but I hated him.

He puts the gag back in Ash's mouth. "Sorry, gorgeous. But I need to talk to Dannie." He stands up and yanks me up off of the ground and immediately whips me back down. I hit the ground with a painful thud and feel my shoulder crack.

I decide to take a risk. It might not pay off but I'm desperate to get Ash out of here alive, and I'm not taking whatever kind of pill that is. I close my eyes and pretend to be unconscious, to not have the strength to fight, staying as still as possible. I feel a heavy slap on my cheek.

"Nope, no time for bullshit." He saw right through it.

There's no avoiding it now. We are getting out of this goddamn room, even if I have to kill Eric to do it. I open my eyes and frantically scan the room. I'm lying on the floor, and Ash was still in the bed, a look of horror on her face as she lies there helpless. It's the same bed Eric kept me in all those years ago. I don't know how I'll be able to sleep in a bed ever again now that these nightmares have become real, and always have been real.

He's looking at me curiously, his eyes asking me silently what my next move is. Shaking, my eyes meet Ash's. She's crying, trying to speak, but unable to get any words out. I attempt a smile and mouth, "It's going to be okay." Eric growls and pins me against the ground, my injured shoulder yelling at me.

My mind goes back to the first time I was here. The smell, the itchy quilt, the pillows wet from tears. I close my eyes again and breathe in and out. In and out. He presses down harder and pulls at my shirt.

Goddamnit. It's going to happen again. I should have texted Rosa on my way here. I should have paused, just for the few seconds it takes to send a message. I should have called the police. There were a billion things I could have done that were smarter than what I'd done, but here I am, in worse trouble than I could have imagined.

Eric slips his hand under my shirt and slowly trails it upward. I'm such an idiot. I hadn't swooped in to save the day. What made me think I could? I probably made things worse. Here I am, trying to keep myself calm when my brain is *screaming* and forcing me to remember things I was desperate to forget.

His hand moves between my breasts and up to my neck. I can still see the keychains dangling over my face all those years ago, and the way his body felt against mine, moving back and forth, harder and harder the more I cried out in pain.

"Why are you doing this again? And why Ash? You could've left her out of this. Cut your losses and left town after you attacked me. But you stayed. Why?"

"Because I had to. You pissed me the fuck off. You hated when I touched you." He points over to the bed, his finger shaking. "You rejected me twice. At the restaurant, then here. You *hated* me. The same way everyone does. After all the things I did, and how I spent my entire life trying to make my mother proud. The way Ashlin ended up rejecting me. All women just hate me and I can't stand it!" He covered his eyes and let out a guttural yell and rolls over, lying on his side, like a child in a tantrum.

My eyes narrow. "So this is because Mommy didn't hug you enough. You had to hurt me, and other people, because you had a terrible mom. Newsflash, asshole. So did I, and I've never raped anyone."

"I've done more than that. Things you couldn't possibly imagine. That's how angry you made me. Their blood's on your hands, Dannie."

I wait for him to go on, wondering what he meant. Oh my god. He killed all those women. He's really is Vance. I keep waiting for him to explain, my whole body shaking. The memory of the shaking keys flashes in my head. I look into Ash's eyes. We exchanged more sentiments in a single glance than we'd ever done in words. I said it all, each word I'd said in the text, and she responded with kindness and something else I couldn't place.

My hands tremble and my heart can't stop racing. I'm almost at the point again where breathing is becoming a challenge. A sharp pain stabbed me in the chest, trying to smash my heart into a million pieces. But I refused to look at Eric, because that meant looking away from Ash, and she was the only one keeping me sane. She tries to speak through the gag, her tired eyes simultaneously trying to reassure me.

My thoughts are going a thousand miles a minute. I wonder if I can get to Ash before he does. He's still on the ground having a fucking pity party. I'm glued to the floor, paralyzed by fear. But I will *kill* him if he hurts Ash the way he'd violated me. Rage building, I let him lie there, hoping he doesn't get back up. That he'd give me even one more minute. There weren't any other great options.

Facing away from me, he says, "You thought you were so sneaky with your little flirtations, but I noticed. Probably other people did, too, you were just so wrapped up in yourself that you didn't care. Or drunk. Does Ashlin know about that? The drinking and the pills you get from Marco?"

"She does. Maybe not the Marco part," I say, between breaths serrated by anxiety, "For the record, I tried to hide it as much as I could because I was ashamed. Do you know why?" One more look at Ash.

"Why?"

"Because a few years ago, something happened to me. I couldn't remember what it was but I could feel it. My entire body could, my soul, every single day. So I drank. I took pills. And guess what?"

"What?" He gets up and crouches down next to me, a newfound fear in his eyes. He lifts one of his hands a few inches off of the ground, as if prepared to strike me.

"I remembered that I got hurt by a disgusting waste of oxygen."

He pummels me, blow after blow, each one harder than the last. I can hear Ash moaning with fury, her breath so heavy until the pill finally does its trick, and I lie there, bleeding, taking the hits for her.

"You know why I never took your keychain? Like I did the others?"

I attempted a whisper but my mouth was filled with blood.

"Because I was ashamed to. Ashamed I ever touched you."

Chapter 24

Charlie

I stare at them, sitting on my desk like a daily memo from the Chief. Except they were enclosed in an evidence bag. The keychains. That's the reason I do this, the idea of being able to give hundreds of people closure. I'd been wrapped up in this mystery for so damn long, I was worn out. I even thought about planning a trip to visit my nieces and nephews and hug the shit out out of them when this is all done, and put flowers on my dad's grave back home with my mom. Maybe I'll go to the beach. Somewhere warm and tropical.

I call Chris over from an adjoining room. "Hey, I could use a second brain."

He jogs over into my office and whispers, "And a first." After a beat, "You've been missing out on an opportunity here. I told you where I was staying."

I scoff. "I've got enough on my plate. I don't need a manchild that I have to wake up and make Cocoa Puffs for."

"Point taken. What's going on, Lieut?"

"I've got this guy. Vance Michaels. I think it's an alias. He has enough docs to buy a local property but nothing else. No school records, no social media presence. People his age usually at least have a Facebook or Instagram. But nothing. Will you help me scan through some pictures in VICAP? Vance Michaels doesn't have a record, but whoever he really is might. He looks so familiar, but I'm so bogged down by the murder cases my brain is fried."

"Sure," he says, nudging me out of my chair and clicking the VICAP icon on my computer. I head over to my coffee maker. "What are the search parameters?"

I stop to think then say, "Choking, strangulation, homicide, assault, domestic abuse, possibly lives or has lived and operated in the Chicago area. He has the brightest blue eyes I've ever seen."

Chris sucks on his teeth and types it all into the system. After four or five minutes of scanning he takes a pause. "Lieut, your brain *must* be fried."

I rub my hands over my eyes and say, "No kidding, there's not enough caffeine in my life. Or sex."

He raises an eyebrow. "I can help you there. And with the caffeine. I'll buy the next coffee. But you need to come look at this." I walk back over and lean over the desk. My jaw dropped open and my breath caught in my throat.

"That's him. The domestic I took. She told me his name. I don't know why I didn't put two and two together. I should have done a more thorough look sooner."

"You need a vacation. And sex."

I roll my eyes. "I'm going to take one when I close these cases, visit some family. Shit, Eric Michael Anderson. It's the eyes. He has darker black hair in the DMV photo, but it's him. Vance is Eric." I pick up my phone and dial a three digit extension. After a minute, I say, "Phil, I need you to follow up on a lead. My domestic, Ashlin, the girl from the real estate agency with the missing boyfriend. We don't have eyes on her either. Her friends are worried. But it's him, this Vance Michaels guy is the missing boyfriend, Eric. Can you swing by the vic's place? They live together. I'll text the address. Thanks."

I let out a deep exhale. "Okay, Phil's gonna check out the apartment. Dannie, the friend, already looked for Ashlin there, and no dice, but maybe Eric went back. Maybe he's gotten stupid."

"And this is the guy you think is good for all the murders?" Chris asks, a finger in his mouth as he chews at a cuticle.

"He has to be. Or at least, needs to be questioned. He owns the house where the keychains were found, and now he beat up on his girlfriend. That can't be a coincidence. Let me try Dannie again and see if they've had any luck finding Ashlin. If not, I'm heading over to the Wayne Ave house and kicking the goddamn door in."

"Without a warrant?"

"Probable cause is a murky body of water." I send out the text to Phil, and then dial Dannie's number. It's a minute or so of endless ringing before I say, "Dannie, it's Charlie. Any word on our girl? Call me back when you get this." My eyes plead with Chris, my heart filled with worry for two people I barely know. I really do need a vacation.

"You call the DA just in case. Her friend Dannie's not picking up either. Looks like we're busting some doors apart. You in?"

Him

Eric

Now

My body feels a strange sense of calm as I pound Dannie's face. She had to say it, didn't she? She had to call me that. It made me so goddamn angry, but now she's getting what she deserves. My blood courses furiously through my veins, but I'm strong and grow more so with every blow.

I never wanted to upset Ashlin so much. I *had* used her to get back at Dannie, that had been the long game. But after some time, I'd actually grown fond of her. I love how optimistic she is, and how much she cares about people. That was until I found out how much she cares about Dannie. I'm tired of being in second place.

Dannie's right eye is already swollen shut, her lip split, her face black and blue. When I'm done, I stand up and stare at her. Ashlin's passed out so I'm not too worried. She'd fought so hard, and the drugs finally won.

This time Dannie won't get away. She's too broken to even get off the floor, let alone run out of the house. Now, she might have even the smallest taste of what I feel like. I've been broken inside for so long. I'm not about to be humiliated by her ever again. Unfortunately, Ashlin would have to suffer the consequences. It's sad when I sit and think about it.

A waste of oxygen. How dare she call me that? My mind drifts back to the last time I spoke with my mother.

"I just want to help. I can take you to meetings, and we can get you the help you need."

Her voice had been measured, trying to steady itself against the drunken stupor. "Get me help? When was the last time anyone tried to help me?"

"We've been trying, mom. For years. You won't listen to reason."

"Listen to reason? Like how we told you to apply to Harvard, really make something of yourself. You say you're doing alright for yourself now, but you could have made better use of your dad's name. Our name."

"You know what? I'm sorry, okay? I'm sorry I hurt you. But I *am* doing alright, and I won't apologize for that. I did it all on my own."

"I didn't ask you to do that, you know. We handed it all right to you, and you threw the chance away like it was nothing. Like we taught you nothing growing up." She took an audible chug from a bottle. "And you know what? I regret it every second of the day, being your mother. But not like I can take it all back. I thought you'd treat me better than your dad but you were just another disappointment."

She slammed the phone down, and the sound plays in my head years later. I cover my ears to drown it out. It buzzes like a swarm of cicadas and I can't make it stop.

Dannie has that same attitude. She doesn't even care how many lives she ruins. Everyone's a piece of shit in some way, I guess. We all breathe the same poisoned air, and none of us deserve any better than anyone else. I've spent my whole life learning that and it was never more obvious than it is now. I stand over Dannie's body and spit on her.

A shine catches my eye. It reflects off the small sliver of light leaking through the curtains. It's so small, I almost hadn't noticed.

One of her keys was hanging out of her pocket.

I didn't add anything of hers to my collection back then, but maybe it was time. I take the pocket knife I always carry with me. I'm so close I could reach out and grab it. Not like she would fight back. Instead, I flip open the knife. With delicate strokes, I run the blade against her hand. Once, then twice. Blood seeps out of the cuts. A bloodied key would be even better.

Oh shit. Someone's here.

There's banging at the front door like someone was trying to break in. I drop the knife and gasp. The noise downstairs stirs Dannie from her stupor. We could hear someone yelling on a bullhorn, some woman, "Eric Anderson? We've got a warrant for your arrest, and we are coming in." The thuds against the door continue. "Put down whatever weapon you might be holding, and lie down, face on the ground, hands in front of you."

My head swims as I think about how I can get out of this. I close the knife and run to the side window. I jerk it open. Wood splinters downstairs as the door finally cracks. Boots hurry their way into the foyer and up the stairs.

I take one last look at Ashlin who was still asleep, and at Dannie, bleeding on the floor and crying. And I jump out of the window.

Chapter 25

Charlie

Now

Rosa pulls up in an Uber just as the wheels of my squad car screech against the curb. She runs toward the front steps, and Phil holds her back. She fights back. "Let me through, you piece of shit. Let me through."

I hold a hand up for silence, my finger to my lips, then return the hand to my gun. In my other hand, I hold a bullhorn. I signal for two uniforms and Chris to approach the door. Chris starts kicking at it near the handle, the wood taking a long time to give.

My cheeks burn with fury thinking about all the lives Eric stole, all the women he'd hurt. I didn't have enough concrete evidence yet, but I know. Just like I know I'm made for the adrenaline running through my veins as I open my mouth and press it against the bullhorn.

"Eric Anderson? We've got a warrant for your arrest, and we are coming in. Put down whatever weapon you might be holding, and lie down, face on the ground, hands in front of you."

A few more kicks and Chris is in. He barks at the uniforms to stay outside with Phil and Rosa. I'm glad he's there as the two of us run in, our boots clapping against the old floorboards.

Is Dannie here, too? I sprint up the stairs, Chris right behind me. I pray to God they aren't. What could have triggered this level of rage in Eric?

We make it to the top of the stairs, and I hear Ashlin whimpering in a nearby room. We run in, and can't believe what we see.

***

"He's running, Phil. Get after him and have the officers set up a perimeter around the surrounding blocks. Tell one of them to contact the CTA. And put a BOLO out on him and his car." I know he understands the urgency. I hear him huffing and puffing as he sprints toward the yard before he even lets the button on the walkie talkie go.

My fingers shake as I untie Ashlin, waking her from what appears to be a drug-induced sleep. The poor woman's wrists are bruised and I think one of them might be sprained, if not broken. "It's alright, it's alright. The medics are headed up to help Dannie, and get you checked out, too." I can hear them heading up, rolling up a wheeled stretcher.

Dannie has rolled over and is trying to talk. I sit down next to them and take their hand. "Try not to talk. Your dumbass is lucky you're not missing any teeth." The joke makes me feel shitty, and I choke back a sob.

But Dannie smirks, then grimaces. Their face is all black and blue, and they would no doubt have quite a hard recovery ahead. Could Eric be the guy? Did these two really have to pay the price for his brokenness?

Three EMTs enter, one heading to Ashlin, and two to Dannie. After checking Dannie's vitals, they lift them onto the stretcher and secure them. As they wheel them away, Ashlin follows with the other EMT. She's unsteady on her feet, but she's going to be okay. Physically anyway.

Ashlin looks back at me, right behind her. "Is Dans going to be okay?" Her voice trembles and her eyes doe-like. I've seen the look before. I saw it in myself when I first started seeing Chris. The flushed cheeks, wide eyes, the look of anticipation and hope.

"Yeah, I think so." I pick up my walkie as I make my way down the stairs, and watch the two get put into an ambulance, Rosa and Ashlin insisting on riding with Dannie. Phil answers, and I say, "Any luck?"

"No, Lieut. That motherfucker was fast. He jumped and took off. Must have had help nearby, a getaway car. We have officers combing the area and doing door to doors. I called CTA. We'll find him."

I nod to myself and say, "Thanks, Phil. Good work." Ugh. Another lead gone, our best one. Maybe we'll find him. Maybe we won't. Still, it was information to add to the board and to convey to the families, and that counts for something.

I barely finish talking to Phil when I get a call, this time from a uniform who I sent to patrol the neighborhood for a sign of Eric. "Yeah?" I say.

"I don't know if this is relevant. I know we're looking for Eric Anderson. But I just found a dude on the corner of Southport and Fullerton. Adult male, estimated late twenties, early thirties. EMTs on the way, if you could head out, too."

"Be right there."

What now? I get in my car and turn on the lights and siren. I rush through the few blocks it takes to get there, and speeds up to the curb. I leap out of the car and over to the young man. "Is it him?" But it obviously isn't, as I stand over him. A cop is keeping pressure on a decent stomach wound.

Poor guy. The alley's dark, a known hang out for drug deals. He's a Hispanic male, a gash in his gut, no sign of the weapon nearby. His eyes are open, stuck in surprise. He's trying to talk and all he can get out is, "He finally did it."

Phil comes up behind me as the ambulance loads up the man and says, "What this about? Coincidental timing. Looks like a similar sized knife as the one Eric cut Dannie with. Should we assume it's related?"

"I don't know. Dannie does have some cuts to her, but we won't know for sure until they're both examined." First, the women by the rivers. Then Ashlin and Dannie. Now, this kid. Couldn't be more than thirty. What does he have to do with it?

I take a glove out of my pocket, put it on, and pick up the vic's phone. It lies next to him on the sidewalk, screen cracked, but still usable. I have him tell me the passcode before he gets taken away. I click on his texts. When I see who his ICE contact is, I can barely breathe. What the fuck? My hands are shaking as I slip it into a bag Phil's passing to me.

The man's emergency contact is Rosa. Dannie and Ashlin's friend.

Chapter 26

Dannie

3 Days Later

Ash holds up a mirror to my face. "I really don't need to see this," I say. My voice is weak and my eyes are heavy. I haven't been able to sleep much the past few days, despite the pain meds given by the nurses. I asked for as few meds as possible. I'm determined to stay clean this time.

"But look at how much improvement you've made. And how much easier it is to talk."

I sigh and look into the small mirror Ash had taken out of her purse, normally used to apply make-up. She's right, I guess. The dark mess my face had been when I was admitted was now turning into lighter shades of brown and green. My nose was bandaged and reset, and my eyes are slowly losing some of the swelling.

"I still look like hell."

"More like... purgatory," Ash says with an upward inflection, attempting a smile.

"I guess," I say and take her hand. She hadn't left my side the entire time, apart from when she was getting looked at and getting her sprained wrist and finger bandaged. "I don't even know what to say. You've been here with me the whole damn time."

Ash clears her throat. "Well, the nurse said Marie's going to be here in like an hour. She wants to set up regular *twice* weekly appointments." I roll my eyes. "I know, I know," Ash continues. "But you made this commitment to yourself. Therapy, AA, NA, all of it."

"I made it to you," I say, daring myself to rub the back of Ash's hand with my thumb.

"You need to make it for yourself. I'll be here regardless." She barely has time to finish her sentence when a cacophony of hurried Spanish emanates from the hallway.

"Mama, you're gonna spill the soup before we even get there."

I smile as Rosa, Mama, and a nurse burst into the room. The nurse says, "I don't know how up for visitors you are, but I couldn't hold this one off." She nods over at Mama.

Rosa shrugs. "You know how she is."

Mama scoffs. "How I am. Dannie is my child, same as you. They might not have come out of me, but when they're sick I bring them soup."

Ash steps aside, so Rosa and Mama can sit beside me and set the soup down. I close my eyes and take a big inhale. "Oh my god, that smells amazing. Chicken and rice?"

"Your favorite, corazón. And Rosa brought muffins."

"She knew how gross the food is here, from my multiple texts," says Ash. "Thanks. And Rosa…" Their eyes met, and a tear rolled down both of their cheeks.

"I know, love. But he's going to be okay. No internal bleeding. I don't know how he ended up mixed up in all of this. Lieutenant Carlson says she has people following up on his military connection to Eric. I just… I thought I could save him. And now look what happened. He could have died."

"You don't need to save everyone," I say. "Your friendship's done wonders for me over the years. It might not seem like it, but it's true. And I'm going to make more of an effort at a *sober* friendship with him. Now, tell me more about this soup and the muffins."

Mama shoves Rosa out of the way and starts to lay out the food on my bedside tray, rolling it across my body. "Made it special this morning, and Rosa got the muffins from a café. Even though I *told her* I could have made them myself."

"It was on the way," Rosa says with a slight rise in tone. "Jesus. Well, anyway, have a muffin. There's enough for you, too, Ashlin, if you want."

I look over at Ash and hand her a muffin. She erupts in a giggle.

"It's a muffin, sugar plum. Not a knock-knock joke." I wave it left and right, eyebrows raised until she takes it.

"Thanks. Lemon poppyseed is my favorite."

The four of us talk while Ash and I eat, talk about Marco's recovery, the family, and anything positive we can think of, making difficult attempts at laughter. It will be a long time before jokes come easy to me, and things feel normal again. But I'm thankful for all of them, and for Charlie. Without her perseverance, I don't know where I'd be.

"I'm really fucking pissed, you know," Rosa says.

"Language, mija!"

I smirk again. "What did I do this time?" I ask through a small bite of a muffin. The bites are slow, but the pain in my mouth is getting better as the days pass.

"You ran in there like goddamn Chuck Norris." Mama scowls at Rosa. "Like you didn't give a single shit about how any of us felt about you."

Ash nods and says, "Not that I'm *not* grateful, but it was reckless. You had me scared out of my mind."

"I'm aware of how all of you feel about me," I say, with a slight wince as I set the muffin down. With weak arms and busted ribs, I adjust my position on my pillow. "But at the moment, I was more preoccupied with how *I* felt." My face flushes, and so does Ash's.

There was so much I still need to say to her, apart from the now infamous texts I'd sent what felt like an eternity ago. The past few days, the two of us have been so focused on feeling better, that we'd put the topic aside. But it'll come up eventually, and I finally feel ready when it does.

Rosa gives a knowing nod, and says, "Well, we'll leave you to eat, but I'll be back tomorrow to help you get home. Don't go doing any cartwheels and fuck up your ribs again."

"*Mija.*"

"Alright, fine. See you tomorrow, love. I'll text you later to see how you're feeling. And thanks for taking care of my best person, Ashlin. Bill's being a dick about too much time off, and I need the money for Marco's hospital bills and, I hope, rehab. It means a lot."

"Of course," Ash says, her beautiful mouth set in a smile that makes my heart flutter. If I wasn't still in tons of pain, I would've pulled her into a kiss days ago.

One more visitor steps in. As much as I appreciate the support, I'm really fucking tired. And I crave some one-on-one time with Ash. Eventually, we'll have that conversation. I hope it's sooner rather than later.

Charlie comes in with a bag that smells like freshly baked donuts. I stare incredulously at another bag of food, and Charlie smiles. "Get it? Donuts? I'm a cop. I'll cut you some slack since you're pretty banged up. It was a good joke."

"It was passable. But thanks, Charlie. I appreciate it."

"Anything for my Dannie and Ashlin." That's something I had come to learn about Charlie over the past few days. She cares about the people involved in her cases. The victims mean everything to her. And that means everything to me. "I hope the visit isn't too much. Just wanted to see how you were."

"I'm hanging in there. I'm going home tomorrow, I think. They want to do one more scan on my ribs, just to be sure. And make sure I can get around okay, even with Ash's help."

Her voice is chirpy and bright. "They're going to stay with me until they're feeling better. I might even cook."

Charlie laughs, and I risk some flirtation. "I might need help in and out of the shower, too."

"All right, well, I can see I've overstayed my welcome," Charlie says awkwardly, and heads for the door. "Take care of yourself, Dannie. You, too, Ashlin. Therapy does wonders. I know from experience."

I can't imagine the visions Charlie took to bed with her at night, and the emotional toll her job takes on her. Real estate photography had ended up proving bad enough.

"Thanks, I'll keep you posted."

Charlie left with a salute. Ash turns to me. "Help in and out of the shower. Oh my God." She bursts into laughter. After a pause, she says, "Wait, really? I honestly hadn't thought about that."

"You are now, aren't you?"

Chapter 27

Rosa

3 Days Later

A tear rolls down my cheek as I flip through pictures on my phone. Marco with his arm around me, making a dorky face. Marco and Tony in better days. Our last family picture before things got bad with his substance misuse. At least he's healing now but, Jesus. I almost lost him.

Why? Why did he have to get himself so caught up in this? I continue going through the few boxes Tony brought over from his and Marco's apartment while Marco remained in the hospital. At least Tony's out of the picture now for good. Small miracles.

I can't get that question out of my head. Why would Eric do something like this?

I knew Eric occasionally bought pills from him, and that they had served together, and one of their other buddies went AWOL, but that was the extent of my knowledge. Eric had been an asshole, but also a rapist. And then a murderer. What the fuck?

I need a break. Looking at Marco's meager possessions has been too hard on me. Mama's watching TV in the living room, and I'm sitting cross-legged on my bed. I lay my head down on my fluffy pillow and close my eyes. There's so much to plan for to get Marco well again. I'm going to need to work overtime to help with all of this. Tía's finally speaking to him after we nearly lost him, but they're still in a rocky place.

I have a massive list. Should he move in with me permanently? It's a one bedroom so where would he sleep? Could I help him get into a good rehab, or even afford one? I need to help him patch things up with people. Maybe we'll have a family dinner. Food *is* our primary love language. Mama could probably help with all of this. Dannie and Ashlin are too emotionally drained for much else, and I wouldn't dare ask after all they went through. I had to keep tabs on them, also. I put my arms over my eyes and another tear slips out.

I'm taking this all on because my aunt and uncle are struggling too much. They stopped speaking to Marco a couple of years ago when his addiction got bad and he started dating Tony. I'm the person he's closest to, so how could I not do anything I can to help? It was just another thing I felt compelled to do for the sake of the family, forget about my own damn mental health.

After a brief nap, I get back to work. I have one more box to look through. I find a shirt I bought him on a family vacation a long time ago. All of that seems so long ago, the times without awkward silences, blatant ignorance, forced laughter when really, we're all broken inside.

I open the box, and there's an envelope on top. It's labeled, *For Ro— Love, Marco.* My breath catches in my throat, and I slide my finger into the back to open it. I can't get it open fast enough but I don't want to damage whatever was inside.

I cover my mouth and begin to read. I didn't want to cry and make Mama upset.

Ro, hey. If you're reading this, things have gotten really bad. Kinda cliche, I guess. Is there an accent mark in cliche? Probably. Whatever. Anyway, this is pretty hard to write. And I've thought for a long time about whether I would ever tell anyone. But if I could trust anyone, it would be you. So, you know how I left Afghanistan and came back all fucked up? I let everyone think it was all the shit I saw there, and that was part of it. But the rest of it was a lot worse. Worse in a different way, I guess.

You know that asshole outed me, Ro. In one of the worst places to do that. They say it's gotten better, and maybe it has a little, but it still has a long way to go. The three of us got into a fight, him, me and Kyle. Then Kyle called me the antigay f-word, and I don't wanna talk about the rest. But ever since then Eric and I haven't been tight. Despite all that Oorah BS. We'll never be friends again, and we were both pissed we'd let it get that far. We risked our careers and freedom over a stupid fight. He wanted to get into business and be some fucking big shot.

They never found Kyle, and it keeps me up at night. It keeps me using. He wasn't a terrible guy. Not really. Just coulda been raised better. Can't fault a guy for that. It was just a bad moment that led to a bad decision that led to all this shit I'm in. It's the same reason Eric's such a prick. One of the reasons, anyhow. I hate what happened there, even more than I hate Eric for outing me. The worst part is, I know I can't take it back, and it haunts me every damn day. I can't bring Kyle back. Maybe I'll be ready to talk about it someday.

I'm sorry. I'm sorry I'm probably super fucked up now. I'm sorry I can't stay clean. Sorry for being such a failure. Sorry for all of it. I just want you to know, you're the best person in my life, Ro. You always have been, and I'll never be able to repay you. Love, Marco

My body's in torment, trying to process Marco's letter. I clutch it to my chest. It kills me. I'm always the person in the family to put everyone first. Covering for my sisters, for Marco, paying for things I can't afford just to feel like I have some value in my huge chaotic family. And now, I'm going to put Marco first one more time, even if it means going broke.

I pick up my phone, fingers shaking. When the familiar voice on the other end picks up, I say, "Hey Marco. How are you feeling today? Can I come by in a bit?"

Chapter 28

Ashlin

A few weeks later

Dannie's head lays on my shoulder. It's been an awful day. Dannie's moods are out of whack, of course. Totally understandable.

They're doing their therapy, which makes me happy. Both of us are going twice a week. I'm even going back to work next month. Well, I'm starting with catching up on about a billion emails and working my way back up to face-to-face interaction.

Dannie hasn't been able to pick up their camera again. It breaks my heart. Dannie's camera is à part of them, like a vital organ, and now they've just cast it aside. Marco's injury, getting hurt because of what Dannie considers something that was their fault—even if it wasn't—has made everything worse.

I stroke Dannie's hair, soft after a bath. They've been growing it out, and it suits them. The cropped hair did, don't get me wrong. But the new growth seems to make Dannie happy. My fingers move slowly back and forth, and I hear Dannie groan.

"What's wrong?" I ask.

"Life, generally. I feel so numb, and blank, and like I never want to speak to another person ever again."

"I'll go take that chicken out of the crockpot then," I say, matching Dannie's tone, but not meaning it.

Dannie sits up. That's easier now that they're fully healed. Physically at least. Their ribs and nose are doing better. I made damn sure of that by calling Eric's family and demanding that they pay for Dannie's medical bills and therapy. They're totally loaded, so it wasn't a problem, and their family lawyer found the situation reasonable. The emotional part is going to take more time. Dannie looks at me, their dark eyes piercing my green ones, staying there for a moment or two longer than would have been comfortable a few months ago.

Nothing's happened between us, apart from the occasional hand-holding, and we still do need to talk about the text messages. Dannie brought it up when we got home after they were discharged, but I want to wait. There had been *so* much emotional bullshit to sift through, and I wanted to be in a better place before we added that to the mix.

But it's time, I think. There's been so much energy charging between us the past several weeks that it's hard to put it off any longer.

Dannie lowers their eyes and says, "Listen, I know you weren't ready, but can we talk about the texts?" They've always had a way of reading my mind.

"Of course. Thanks for giving me time. It's just... it's a lot to process."

"I know. I should have said it all in person. A long time ago. But I was terrified."

I cover Dannie's hand in mine. My heart is at full speed, pounding in my chest stronger than it ever has before. Maybe even stronger than when Eric held us captive, as weird as that sounds. I feel something happening. I don't know what, but I finally have the courage. "You don't have to be scared anymore." I slide my hand up from Dannie's hand to their face and rest it on their cheek, caressing the smooth skin that used to be covered in bruises. A face that had always held hidden pain. Dannie's eyes close, and they sigh.

I close my eyes, too. I can hardly breathe, but not from nerves, from readiness. I'm so ready. About damn time.

I inch my face closer to Dannie's and press my lips against theirs. It is slow and soft, and Dannie is patient, considering how long they've waited. Our mouths spend a minute or two getting used to the feeling. They graze tentatively, learning each other's language. It's totally unexpected. I never saw this coming when I met Dannie all those years ago, but I feel whole, like my mouth has been meant to be against theirs my entire life.

Our lips keep telling us to explore each other, to not let go of this feeling, and we listen. My breathing becomes heavier, matching Dannie's, and I don't want to separate from them. Ever. If the last month has taught us anything, it's to not take anything for granted. It's easier than I expected, and I give them one more kiss before we stop. I can feel a tear rolling down my cheek.

Dannie flounders for words, completely bewildered. "Damn, Ash."

I laugh. "Yeah, same." It wasn't scary at all. It felt natural, like my mouth had come home. We both smile, and I shake my head back and forth. "Could have been a fluke."

Dannie tosses it over in their head, mouth set in a stern frown. "You could be right. I don't like admitting when I'm wrong, but I'll give you that."

"Do you think it needs further testing?" My leg grazes Dannie's. We're both wearing pajama shorts, as the pre-summer heat wave has rolled into Chicago and the air conditioning units are taking time to catch up. We turn to face each other, and I slide my leg in between Dannie's, a slow heat coursing through my body.

This time the kiss is more sure of itself, frantic even, and it lasts twice as long. Dannie teases my tongue with hers, and I find myself moaning. The longer we kiss, the more I realize I want more. I want all of Dannie, as much as Dannie is willing to give me.

"We don't have to, you know," Dannie says. "You've been through a lot."

"What about you? You've been through it, too."

"You're always worried about me. I'll be okay. Think about yourself for a change."

The statement doesn't need an answer, not one with words. By now, Dannie and I can read each other like our favorite books, as voraciously and intensely. I swing my leg over Dannie's lap and sit there, facing them.

Dannie's eyes are deep pools of... something. A mixture of longing and fear. I don't know what Dannie's afraid of, but I would do whatever it takes to make it go away. I kiss Dannie, with the kind of love I had always wanted from someone.

Hours later, when we wake up under my sheets, I run my finger up and down Dannie's arm. Dannie rolls over and smiles, saying, "Definitely wasn't a fluke."

We interlace our fingers and lie there for another hour or so, talking, and just enjoying periods of quiet.

Chapter 29

Dannie

The Next Day

That was the best day of my life. I stretch my arms over my head as the morning sun peeks in through Ash's blinds. Every limb on my body aches, not in an unfavorable way, and I take a while to savor it.

It's been a good decision to make Ash's apartment home. Things are so much brighter here, full of life. On the days I'm not with Rosa, or Ash, or conning Mama into coming for a visit, I don't feel as alone. I'm not in as much emotional solitude as I used to be. In fact, I don't have much alone time at all anymore. And oddly enough, that sits just fine with me.

The apartment has people coming and going like the revolving doors at a department store. Rosa comes over for movie nights, and when she needs a shoulder to cry about the ongoing drama with Marco. It makes me happy, surprisingly, given the introvert I am. I'm just glad to see Rosa and Ash bonding more. Sometimes, she brings Evan for board games and mocktails. I've been completely sober for weeks, and I'm grateful my friends are so supportive. Ash's always coming up with ideas for new alcohol-free drinks, giving them corny names that make me roll my eyes and hold back tears at the same time.

Mama is the only one in Rosa's family consistently speaking to her. She'd violated a code that was unspoken and thrust upon her when she was born—family above all else. She supported Marco's sexuality and, according to them, enabled his drug use for so long. Which is bullshit, that last part. And now she's still taking Marco's side. That's how good of a person she is. He's doing a bit better, and I told her they'll come around.

"They just need time to process," I say later that day, sitting in a booth with Rosa at Flora's. Ash's trying to create a better work from home set-up today, plus trying to catch up on the shitstorm of emails she's missed over the past month or so. That's the longest I've ever seen her neglect her inbox.

Rosa sighs. "I know. I just miss them. I'm glad I have Mama, but I miss my stupid sisters, and the boys, and even Tía... I miss my circle, you know?"

"You've got me. And Ash. That's like a triangle, I guess."

"Good to see you've been brushing up on your geometry on your time off work. What's next for Dannie the photographer?"

"I think real estate photography has run its course. Under the circumstances. Ash said I should have a go at shooting for a magazine. Something artsy, like I always wanted to do. Maybe travel a little, or some other wholesome shit."

"That'd be good for you, love. Chicago's the best city in the world, but there are other ones worth viewing through that lens of yours. You could turn it into a book one day. All about your life, pain, your rediscovery, and healing through your work."

"That's not a bad idea," I say, before taking a sip of my coffee. My phone buzzes. "Text from Ash," I say, without looking at what I know is an inquisitive and annoyed look from Rosa. Rosa and Ash are in a good place, but Rosa still cherishes her solo lunches with me, and ribbing me about being *in loooooove*, as she puts it. "Sorry, let me just see what she says. It looks like the emoji section is having an orgy."

My eyes scan the text, and I cringe.

"What's up?" Rosa says. "There a Kate Spade sale?"

I give her a reproachful look, and Rosa holds up her hands by way of apology. "No, she got invited to a wedding. Her cousin's getting married in South Carolina."

"Mazel tov. You hate weddings."

"How did you know she asked me to go?" Dannie asks.

"I know you, and I can tell by the look on your face. It's like a mish mash of excitement, nerves, and that taste in your mouth after you throw up."

I bite my lip. "She wants me to be her plus one. Her family doesn't even know about us yet. And they're... Well, they didn't vote for Biden."

"Just do what's best. For you, for Ashlin. And the two of you. It has to come out eventually, pun intended."

I nod and type out a reply. "Let's see how she likes that." I never thought I'd see the day.

***

On my way back up to the apartment, I plan the rest of the day out in my head. Marie said that could be helpful, adding more structure and predictability. I run through a mental checklist. Edit the pictures of the unhoused people I took this afternoon—which I told them was for a project, and the people were happy to participate. And the pictures from the glitzy parts of Millennial Park this morning. It was an idea I had to start off my new digital photo album, show reality through the eyes of the people it affects, and hope it makes a difference.

Later, Ash is making something amazing for dinner. As I drool at the thought of what she's making, I dig out my keys to go get the mail. I keep the set simple: apartment, mailbox, Rosa's apartment. It'd been a couple of days, so I open our mailbox, a medium-sized bronze rectangle easily lost among the others if not for the number. It's filled with bills and junk, and a letter from Mama. Then I make it to the last one. My heart catches in my throat, and I drop the rest of the mail.

It's addressed to me. And it's from Eric.

TO BE CONTINUED

Acknowledgements

This book has been a dream of mine for a long time. I've loved writing for as long as I can remember, and it's so rewarding to see this come to fruition.

I wrote the book in its entirety, but the entire project was the product of the hard work of so many people. I just typed the words and came up with the story. I have dozens of people I want to thank. If I've forgotten you, please don't take it personally. Let me know, and I'll buy you a drink.

Thank you to my partner, and my two wonderful friends, for letting me know that it didn't sound like a terrible idea for a story. That really gave me the courage to crack away at it.

Thank you to my longtime friend for her help with questions about the real estate industry. I could have googled shit, but I trusted her insight a lot more.

Thank you to my lovely beta readers Justine, Bianca, Ezra, and Brittany for their help. The links will take you to any books they might have written themselves.

Thank you to my editor, Jessica Hayden. She was a dream to work with and can be found on Fivrr. I also want to thank my cover designer Daniel Eyenegho for his amazing work. He can also be found on Fivrr.

Thank you to my psychiatrist and therapists for helping me get out of my own head and do this damn thing. I would never have found the confidence until I met you.

Also, apologies to Nicholas Sparks. At one point a character pokes fun at him, but I really do like his books. Not that he will ever see this, but it felt necessary to say that. I cried my eyes out at "The Notebook."

Thank you to my friends for their support through my, at one point, secret writing project when I was frazzled and not always super present. I love the hell out of you. Not going to name you all here, but suffice it to say you are beautiful monarchs.

Thank you to my friend in New York, and your team. You are one of the bravest people I know, and you've given me so much courage. I might not have been able to realize this lifetime dream of mine without your dedicated help and relentless effort. I wrote this for you, "It will be a long time before jokes come easy to me, and things feel normal again. But I'm thankful for all of them, and for Charlie. Without her perseverance, I don't know where I'd be." I loosely based her on you because she is strong, and a total badass, and because you showed me that we can slay dragons together, even if it takes a long time to find their lair.

Thank you to my partner and babies for understanding how important this was to me. You are more amazing than you could ever know, my loves. Thank you for giving me grace on days that I was cranky because I couldn't think of the word that was on the tip of my tongue. I love you more than I could ever say. There's probably a word for how special you are, but I can't think of it right now.

And a special hug goes out to the people I wrote this for. I wrote this book from a place of immense privilege (racial, financial, familial, etc) and that needs to be acknowledged. So, this is *especially* for those who feel as though they need to hide who they are because they're afraid people won't accept them—either for their mental health status, gender identity, substance misuse, or sexual preference. Also, this is for victims of abuse who are trying to heal. I actually almost killed off Marco. That was a part of the original outline. But I realized, with the help of my editor, that he deserved more than that. He deserves the chance to live his truth as authentically as possible. I also wanted to create a strong protagonist for you. One who ticks a lot of sometimes common boxes: a queer person struggling with self-doubt and grappling with their feelings, who deals with unacceptance and substance misuse, someone with massive amounts of anxiety, but who ends up being the hero of their own story. The world needs to see people like them—like you—and I needed to write this so I could see myself.

If you are reading this, and you can relate to Dannie, or Ashlin, or Rosa, or Marco—who all fight their own battles—this book is for you. All of you strong, beautiful people are going to change the world.

Sources

I have to give credit where credit is due. I did a lot of research to—I hope—accurately portray different aspects of the story. Thank you to all of the writers of this material! Keep on keepin' on.

Ortberg, Daniel Mallory. "How To Become An Undetected Serial Killer." Published September 9, 2014 on the-toast.net.

Heiter, Elizabeth. "Criminals Who Go Dormant… For A While." Published December 30, 2014 on strandmag.com

SSA Morton, Robert J, et al. "Serial Murder: Multi-Disciplinary Perspectives for Investigators." Released on the FBI website by/for the Behavioral Analysis Unit.

Dr. Martens, Willem H.J. (MD, PhD). "The Hidden Suffering of the Psychopath." Published on October 7, 2014 on psychiatrictimes.com

Unnamed Cleveland Clinic medical professional. "Dissociative Amnesia." Last reviewed by site November 23, 2020 on my.clevelandclinic.org

Unnamed Casa Palmera staff members. "How Trauma Affects Your Memories." Published on January 13, 2010 on casapalmera.com

Unnamed Mayo Clinic staff members. "Dissociative Disorders." Publishing date unknown on mayoclinic.org

Written by Dr. Seladi-Schulman, Jill (PhD) & Medically reviewed by Dr. Legg, Timothy J. (PhD, PsyD). "What Is Dissociative Amnesia and

How Is It Treated?" Published on October 12, 2019 on healthline.com

Dream meanings researched on auntyflo.com. I do think dreams mean things. For real.

About the Author

Julian Kennedy is a debut author who lives in the Midwestern United States with their family (a partner and three wonderful kids). They've wanted to publish a book ever since they were a kid, and are psyched to finally realize that dream.

In their spare time, Julian is an avid true crime fan and can be found listening to "their murders," as their skeptical partner always says. They've also been a bookworm since they could walk. They enjoy a wide range of books—from classic literature, to fluffy rom-coms, to true crime, to creepy mysteries. Just about anything with pages will do.

You can find Julian and connect with them on:
authorjuliankennedy.com
Goodreads: Julian Kennedy
Amazon: Julian Kennedy
Twitter: @jkennedy_author
Instagram: @jkennedy_author
Facebook: Julian Kennedy
Pinterest: @authorjuliankennedy

Thank you so much for purchasing a copy of my book. Please, if you enjoyed it, can you do me a couple of favors? First, consider leaving a 5-star rating on Amazon and Goodreads. It's incredibly helpful, so other people find this book and enjoy it themselves. It's much appreciated by new (and seasoned) authors alike, as it helps get more eyes on it.

Also, consider sharing the Amazon or Goodreads link with friends you think might like Dannie's story.

Next, if you are in need of assistance like any of the characters in the book, someone can help you at:

https://www.ptsd.va.gov/
https://www.betterhelp.com/
https://www.thehotline.org/ or Call 800-799-SAFE (7233) They also give you tips if you are concerned about the privacy of your search history.
https://www.rainn.org/resources
https://www.samhsa.gov/find-help/national-helpline
https://www.thetrevorproject.org/

Lastly, please consider donating to an organization very dear to my heart at https://give.thetrevorproject.org/give/63307/#!/donation/checkout

On the anniversary of each of my books' releases, I will be donating a portion of the proceeds to them, as well. A lot of young (and otherwise) LGBTQ+ people are in massive need of our support right now.

Thank you, thank you, thank you, you wonderful people.

All my love,

Julian

Made in the USA
Las Vegas, NV
25 September 2022